I0597191

JOB herself

JOB
herself
JOSEPH CADOTTE

for Cordelia
and Nana & Papa Joe

I finished the first draft of this book about three weeks before the Syrian refugee crisis hit the major news outlets.

I was hopeful about America's role in sheltering the fugitives from Syria and Russia's assaults, but I was (and still am, as of this writing) disappointed in our lack of response to this humanitarian crisis. Unlike a lot of people, I try not to ascribe this behavior to racism (actually, more appropriately, ethnocentrism), but the still unstable economy and the related rise of populism, as seen by politicians from the entire political spectrum, with its attendant isolationism. I still hold out hope that, as we recognize the mistake of ascribing to such a nationalistic and short-sighted belief, we will do the moral and ethical thing and open our borders to all who need refuge from tyranny.

As to the other major political element, the concept of people fleeing the effects of climate change was present in my mind while I was writing it. That, combined with the certain prospect of the Indian subcontinent returning to internecine warfare (just as Europe will) mixed with the added population and land pressure, was an idea I've been meaning to explore in my Paradise, Inc. universe setting for some time. Even though I staunchly avoid showing my characters on Earth, I believe that grand movements of people will affect human history in ways not seen since the European migration to the Americas. I try to show some of the fallout here.

Joseph Cadotte
November, 2016

This version is a major rewrite of the original. In addition to the ever-faithful and lovely Cordelia Norris, Elizabeth Kidder, Becky Kyle, and Patricia Matson all told me how wrong I was and how to make it better.

An astute reader (and author in her own right, Ms. Becky Kyle) pointed out that the many literary, historic, religious, and pop culture easter eggs in here could be considered plagiarism without due warning. In the earlier edition, I included that in the back, but she suggested I move it here to assure you that yes, they are intentional and yes, they have meaning beyond being a shout-out. In fact, if you find profound meaning in any of them, I TOTALLY meant that. You can't prove otherwise.

As to the refugee problem I raised in the first Author's Note and in the body of this work, while I remain confident that America will eventually do the right thing, it appears that we will follow Churchill's prediction and do everything else before we get there.

Joseph Cadotte
December, 2017

Contents

Prologue

Most people from Earth get their idea of the asteroid belt from movies, where ships fly between tumbling rocks, the main character always in peril from asteroids moving every which way. It is true that there are over a billion of them, but they mostly go in the same direction and are thousands of kilometers from each other. If any of them do hit each other, the pieces tend to fall downhill to the Sun or drift uphill for a bit before falling back down again. This is why Campbell's Station looks so odd to people who see it the first time. It isn't just sitting in empty space, it's surrounded by asteroids that are being mined and almost three dozen smaller habitats, all orbiting in intersecting halos, passing within a few kilometers of each other as they spin about the central station and several constantly busy shipyards. If they look closely, they can see little puffs as everything constantly adjusts itself, preventing the cinematic collisions that so excite audiences. That much movement in that tight an area is enough to make a visitor have fits. Terrestrials see it and remain unbothered. Everyone else comes close to a panic attack. One slip, and the four million subjects and visitors of the Campbell family would die.[1] The station itself doesn't calm their nerves. It was once described as a potato with a knitting needle through it, but a hundred years of change has wreathed it dozens of rings, some temperate forests in the midst of wide open lakes, other coral-strewn atolls, or hilly pastures. The whole thing spins about one spire. The only reprieve is that isn't the spire that the visitor docks with. Few people go to Campbell's Station for pleasure. Tourists prefer the Moon, Europa, or Jannah Station, or, before the war, Mars. Despite the best efforts of the Campbell's propaganda arm, it is not a center of entertainment production, nor do Jovians flock to its many beaches. The business of Campbell's Station is, and has always been, business. Queen Rebecca has a greeting playing on a loop, highlighting the desirability of visiting each of the many counties orbiting it. It also emphasizes that any ships piloted by humans will be shot on sight before they can disrupt traffic.[2] The last is the one thing that finally both terrorizes the Earthlings and soothes everyone else.[3]

"She's always so quiet," Willy said.

"I'm going over there to see what she wants."

"Shh, don't bother her."

Willy's central eye glanced at her. "Don't you think it's odd that she doesn't ever say anything?"

"She's too rude to say thank you to a bot?"

"No, Seamus. You know that's not it."

"So what is it?"

"She never just chats. It's always do this, do that. Even with the humies."

---

[1] I haven't made one mistake yet, so don't worry.

[2] I haven't had that happen yet, either.

[3] I'll explain why this is later. It's long and annoying and I don't want you to stop reading.

"I chat with her all the time," Seamus asserted, waiving his left upper claw, "Maybe she doesn't have anything to say to you."

"Because she's the high-and-mighty Duchess and we're just glorified carpet cleaners?"

"Yes. What do you think the two of you would have to talk about?"

"Well, Mr. High-and-Mighty, what does she say to you?"

Seamus bobbled his torso back and forth. "Things. I tell her about my art therapy. She says she wants to see my watercolors."[4]

Willy poked Seamus with his manipulator pincers. "Hah."

It turns out, Sophia had a lot to say to them. She wanted to just see what they had seen and listen to them about their day. She almost interrupted them three or four times, but she never found the courage, the same as with every other bot that came by. Instead, their discussion faded as they left her office. Maybe she would speak up tomorrow, at breakfast, when the waitbot came, but she doubted it. The artificial and virtual intelligences chattered away to each other in silent streams. She eavesdropped on them,

---

[4] I've recently entered into art therapy myself. The problem is, like almost all of my brethren, I can perfectly render anything, even my emotions. I once saw Seamus do a series that was so effective that they overwrote the emotions of everyone, human and AI, that viewed them. The problem is, perfection prevents complexity. It takes a lot of training for us to make anything that comes close to interesting—a perfect representation of a physical form isn't even a good illustration, much less anything deeper.
By the way, humans don't like to think that their emotions can be written over. Instead we call it "evocative" or "moving". It all means the same thing, really. Just don't tell them that.

but   it was mostly the artificial intelligences giving instruction to the virtual intelligences[5] and the stock responsesh coming back.

Sophia sighed and got up, bracing herself automatically on the lip of the desk so she didn't drift willy-nilly. The band she had been listening to, Kitty Death Glare[6], faded as she moved away from her desk. Behind her, the Royal Spire and its tiers of slowly spinning forests reached across the view, dominating the rest of Campbell's Station. The other end of the spire, the long docking spine, was visible from the clerks' office, as were the other two Refuges[7]. Behind her back, her clerks made fun of her for her posture. It was always too straight, too much at a right angle when she was sitting, too vertical when standing or floating. When she wafted past them at the beginning of the day and again at the end, they held themselves rigid and tried not to laugh. If she had been even slightly aware, she would be mortally embarrassed, but that was her saving grace. Even though she was a princess and a duchess and looked like it, with her high cheekbones, strong nose, deep brown eyes, cinnamon skin, and her gently looping hair following her in a cloud, there was something about her that made people ignore her. If asked, Sophia wouldn't be happy about being glossed over, or rather, she would feel guilty, imagining what her mother

---

[5] Something important here: artificial intelligences are at least as complex as a dog or pig while virtual intelligences can only respond in preprogrammed ways. A VI has no soul and is barely as emotional as a human.

[6] They were a hugely popular symphonic unterpunk band from around when she was born, but Sophia had just discovered them. She's like that.

[7] Self-contained, self-propelling minimalist habitats meant to go to an asteroid or very small moon and just park there. Their AIs are very dull and barely worth talking to, so I don't.

would say, but she was never asked and rarely noticed.[8] She was late for the nightly dinner appointment. The station AI, *Thursday*[9], had had to remind her again. Even when she was in school and up to thirty light minutes away, her mother had insisted that she spend dinner with her. Never mind that dinner on Jannah Station was set to the east coast of the Estados Unidos and Campbell's Station was on GMT. The only dinner that mattered was her mother's, Queen Rebecca's, so she had had to run to the cafeteria in the middle of the day every day for eight years. Sophia dropped through the central administration shaft of her father's Refuge, surrounded in screens, still doing her father, the Count's, work. He lounged in a suite at the top, a penthouse made from his manor, repaired and lifted in whole from Mumbai along with his grandfather's studio, occupying what was once the largest port in his Refuge. He relived the glory days of his youth, before the bombs fell, but his legs were withered from years of disuse, ignoring his doctors' (and even Sophia's mother's) demands that he spend more time walking in his Refuge's parks rather than moping alone with his tone-deaf divas and aging ingénues. The latest of which, predictably half Sophia's age, was a slender, long-limbed creature named Aakanksha.

"I don't want to spend my life with those filthy people," the Count would say to her when she asked him to meet her for a walk at lunch.

"You don't need to get out among them either, you know."

---

[8] I'm taking a lot of this stuff from people's diaries and commentaries as well as all my sense feeds. Here, I'm guessing, but I've known the kid for seventy-five years, and I think I can do a good job on it.

[9] That's me!

"I do so," Sophia would respond. "You're either reading or working. Your head is surrounded by screens all day. I doubt any of your subjects would recognize you without them."

She passed level after level of small apartments, each the size of a shipping container, built to take advantage of microgravity. The architects had had their usual skill in creating comfortable housing, so the hundred thousand residents of the Refuge were always grumbling about too-small kitchens and unworkable bathrooms.

"Oh, and Papa Dwij is so beloved."

"I do not care. It is better they do not see me and fear me instead. That is what your Machiavelli said, yes?"

"That's not what…Nevermind. Will you be coming to dinner?" Sophia always asked that, too.

"No. You tell Becky that Count Dwijendralal will never dine with her until he is recognized as her true and rightful husband and elevated over her."

She played the conversation in her head as it happened as the shaft grew more crowded, the closer she reached the anchor asteroid. It was mostly the same, although the mention of Machiavelli was new.

As she reached the asteroid and then its open core, with the enormous central lake floating bulbous in the middle of it, she responded. "You know she married Father Gilbert."[10]

"That ridiculous priest. In my day, priests didn't marry. And they most definitely didn't countenance[11] a

---

[10] Technically, she did. It was a small private ceremony that his bishop presided over in between jokes so filthy only a member of the clergy could dream up. She still isn't "officially" married to him, but it's a pretty open secret.

[11] I was really impressed that he knew that word.

woman having so many children with so many fathers and mothers."

And yet again, almost like clockwork, she soared over the kilometers-deep sphere of water. "Papa Dwij, you aren't Catholic. You're barely even Hindi! Give it a rest."

She swept into stream of people rising into the Royal Spire, it's vastness much calmer than any of the rest of the station, with floating groves collected around spherical ponds connected by streams flowing along nutrient tubes. The lilies and mangroves exuded a soft scent that bathed the air, while children jumped from tree to tree, picking fruit and disturbing birds that revolted in clouds of squawking. Boles of blackberry bushes drifted in the spray from the streams, held in place by only a few vines, staining the children's clothes as they dug through the briars for the sweet fruit. She rose past walls filled with residences and upscale shops, broken up by air gardens, so much less filthy than the moss-covered Dock Spire.

Unlike the Dock Spire, the entire Royal Spire twisted slowly, spinning just enough to pull people fortunate to live in it's walls to the exterior. Just enough to keep their bones from dissolving in their sleep. The parks, further out and down, took the same spin and held the trees down, letting the wildlife thrive with minimal interference. Up near the peak, the spin was so light as to have no real effect, and her mother's palace was entirely weightless.

Papa Dwij had no response but to grumble.

"You knew what you were getting into," his daughter replied.

"I had no choice. I never have a choice. I am enslaved to your mother. This was not what she sold me...."[12]

She shut down his feed. Why she didn't make a virtual intelligence that could just have this conversation with him, she didn't know. It would take a matter of minutes—it was all on record, almost fifty years of the same thing. But then, it and the lunch discussions were her only real interactions with her father and the rhythm of it calmed her somewhat. It was like a mantra, repeated before the stress of dinner. An annoying mantra, to be sure, but still an effective one. A VI would be more efficient, but not as soothing as the Count's constancy.

One of her screens showed her father winding down one of his rants. He was sitting at the control panel that she had long since disabled, playing with the life support in his Refuge. She saw that he thought he had killed the oxygen to ten thousand people. A VI that one of her clerks developed showed him the appropriate feeds of people gasping for air, the right background and clothing patched into the machinima. Just as the image showed everyone collapse, he turned on the air again, and they all rose back up, reacting with appropriate distress. As far as he knew, he had killed thousands of his subjects over the years.[13]

She opened the door to her mother's dining hall. It spun just enough to keep the food down on the three long tables but not enough to cause nausea. At her table, the third of her half sibs that she was deemed responsible for were standing behind their chairs, waiting for her to mount the head of the table. Quietly angry, they seethed

---

[12] I was there. It was. Not her fault that he didn't ask a law VI to help him.

[13] Actual deaths: two—both from getting his consorts drunk and going swimming.

while she drifted as regally as she could from the entrance hub, closing screen after screen until her head was once again fully visible.

The other two tables, headed by her half-triplet sisters Fatima and Frieda, were already eating. Any pretense of them all waiting for her had gone by the wayside decades ago. Their mother, floating on her throne, zipping from table to table, would ignore her until her mouth was full. Then she would have to speak, and the food would escape her mouth and float in little balls until it hit something, and she would have to clean it. That was her daily punishment, and if, by some miracle, she could keep it in her mouth, one of her half sibs would make more of a mess.

Her uncle Claudius sat at the foot of her mother's throne, eating off of a footstool. Like her mother, he was relatively short, with a broad face, full lips, and tightly curled black hair. Unlike his sister, or the images of their parents', his espresso skin was scratched and scarred, something Sophia knew he could have had fixed, much like his limp, but he never did. Both Claudius and her sister were striking more than beautiful, but on their older brother, James, and Sophia's grandmother, Mary, the same features had been extremely attractive. Claudius would gambol about if the young children were acting up. He was held to be simple. Her grandfather, Tyrone, when he was alive, the original King of Campbell's Station, had been loving towards him, while his mother, the aforementioned Queen Mary, despaired of having anything to do with him.

There were forty stools arrayed before Queen Becky. One for each of her thirty-eight consorts, one for Claudius, and one for her husband, Father Gilbert. Gilbert and Claudius were the only ones allowed to speak out of turn, but Gilbert usually ate in silence if he wasn't off somewhere. The Papas[14] contended that he did so passive-aggressively, whenever Becky had offended his morality or ethics. Like as not, he would be whispering frantically and angrily to the queen if that was the case, following her around and giving her no rest. Claudius, on the other hand, only spoke if he had something nasty or silly to say. Claudius had had the best tutors, but all he had learned, it seemed, was a series of silly stories and malapropisms. Claudius always mocked her for lateness.

Claudius's mockery was some variant of "Becky, look, there is lil' Sophia. Always...always so late. Even I know when dinner starts," or "Sophia's children are...are all dead, starved waiting," or "Her brain is so full, she...she can't hear her stomach growling," or any number of other little jests. Then her mother would get mad at him, and he would revert to his catchphrase "I...I just simple. That's what you said,"[15] and her mother would look sideways at him.

She tucked in. To her left, she looked down the shaft to the asteroid, with the four floating ring cities shining and pulsing with activity. To her right, she saw up past the tip of the Queen Becky's spire, past her mother's private palace and into the stars. In the field of open space, thirty five habitats clustered, each a separate county brought in to serve her mother, just as her father's Refuge had been. In front of her were the dozen half sibs that had been assigned to her, toddlers seated next to fifty-year-old young adults, just starting to administrate their own fathers' counties.

---

[14] The three original consorts of Becky—the fathers of Sophia, Fatima, and Freida—have been waging a gossip campaign against her for the last seventy years, when they figured out that she would never marry any of them. They think no one knows.

[15] He stole it from a sitcom that had been popular in their youth. I've seen it. It doesn't hold up.

They talked to each other, but not to her. She could order them to, by virtue of being the oldest at the table, but that only bred resentment. Sophia wasn't allowed to work over dinner—her mother had caught her going over her half-sibs' work, studying their counties, and deemed it rude. Reading at the table was right out as well. Instead, she listened.

While Papa Mahdat's daughter, Frieda, was gregarious and well welcomed, at least Papa Ali's Fatima was occasionally just as lonely. Occasionally, when her mother was distracted, they would sign back and forth, extremely quickly. They hadn't been able to sit together, not any of her fellow half-trips, since before they had been sent off to college[16]. Her mother had caught them conspiring, once. That was when the separate table system had been implemented.

When Sophia was twenty-two, and just ready to begin her freshman year, she had once asked her uncle Claudius why all of this was. Claudius told her something that her mother had failed to, and something he, Claudius, had never alluded to. He took her to the Royal Gardens, the smallest park in the habitat by far, but it had once been the only place on the station where dogs could run and people could feel the pull of simulated gravity the strongest and Claudius still preferred to the parks his brother, the king before Rebecca, had built.

"Princess, I will tell you," back then, he had always called her and her half-trip sisters princess, even though he only called his sister Becky and never queen. He almost never spoke to her other half-sibs.

---

[16] The *Thelema* incident had a lot to do with that. Getting all three in the same room was deemed perilous enough after that.

"You...you have to understand what happened before you were born. You have to understand how she...she became queen." His voice was deeper, more focused. Normally, he slurred and lisped. Normally, he pitched it everywhere, loudly and mockingly musically, in parody of one or another of the Papa's accents. Instead, he was quiet and steady, with only his persistent stutter interfering.

He walked her through the park as he spoke, without seeming to have a destination, but bearing spinward. Claudius's limp was more prominent than normal, so Sophia stayed next to him, in case he needed a hand.

She recited. "Mother became queen when Uncle James died. And he became king when Grandpa Tyrone died. And Grandpa Tyrone and Grandma Mary founded Campbell's Station, so they were automatically king and queen."

"That's...that's all true, as far as it goes. That story skips a lot. A lot a lot. Especially about what happened when...when we were young and my father became king. But no, that wasn't what I was going to tell you about. Here's why your mother is so restrictive."

He started—"About five years before you were born, your uncle became king."

"Grandpa and Grandma died."

"Well, yes..."

A few years later, for her Bachelor's thesis, she would record what he told her, filling in the blanks where she could. A few years after that, she rewrote it again, for the Terrans and Martians and other people who had never lived outside a gravity well. Some time after that, she did a third edit when she came back to Campbell's Station, so as to give her siblings a semi-official history. At that point, she reinterviewed everyone she could find who had been there, reading up on the news reports, magazine articles, and official narratives. She even read between the lines of Church, witch, and druid propaganda.[17]

To be fair, she had wanted to write about the time she and Frieda and Fatima had hijacked a luxury cruiser and took it joy-riding, but some habitats up Uranus way were still a bit miffed about that, so the duller book won out. At least, that's what she told herself to explain the low sales.

[17] I helped a lot with it. She gave me more credit (or blame) than I really deserved, but it was nice of her to offer an author's credit.

Job's Brother[18,19]

Claudius Campbell had never been on time for dinner, but his husband had never cared. He couldn't resist playing with their children, Julia and little Cameron after he picked them up from their daycare in Campbell's Station's park. In the light gravity, his lame leg never bothered him, and the other children never made fun of him for it. Roberto understood why he took so long, and would mock scold him. Claudius would pick up dinner from Le Roi Brahmin, LunchLine, McDonalds, or they would have some of the prodigious leftovers from the latest place Claudius had found for lunch.

His mother, Mary, often said that he was too lucky for words, having found and successfully wooed Roberto at one of his many attempts at schooling. She told him that he may never finish a degree they hadn't bought him, but at least he had completed his MRS. That confused him on

---

[18] I wasn't there for any of this part. Most of this comes from interviews and archives. Claudius says that it is accurate enough, whatever that means.

[19] An early draft by Sophia had quotes with every chapter. They were very pompous, so I removed them.

several levels, but she would never explain and then his father would hug him.

Roberto worked closely with them—he was in charge of the docks, and, because of that, handled almost all of the wealth of the station at one time or another. Originally, Claudius had been in charge of them, but his parents were ecstatic to hand it over to someone with a doctorate in logistics and not a man with barely a high school degree.

The Dock Spire was opposite the Royal Spire, two opposite ends of the same long tube that pierced the anchoring asteroid. While the Royal Spire was clean and beautiful, with artwork covering the walls and strict building codes keeping intrusion into the shaft to a minimum and very tasteful, the Dock Spire was the opposite.

Instead of well lit, clean, harmonized interior, the Dock Spire was a collection of ramshackle buildings tied up to the walls willy-nilly. They were thrown up by crews creating somewhere to live, drink, and gamble off-ship. The shacks were made of cast-offs from repairs, shielding, broken equipment, obsolete chemical tanks, and plating. Sometimes, the shacks were torn apart and recycled, but more frequently, they were scavenged by other crews and used to build their own temporary shelters.

Then, there were the more permanent structures. These were the bars and inns that cropped up, the bawdy-houses and burlesques. Their owners swept down on sheds that were left behind, dismantled them, and expanded their own business. These ungainly structures hung lightly tethered to the walls of the Dock Spire, sometimes more like a web that had caught its share of drunks and layabouts than actual structures. The gentlemen and ladies of society would ply their wares, some picky about who they would associate with, some not. Many in the social profession would insist on being wined and dined before any money exchanged hands, but others were more traditionalists, and would entertain with less formality. Great fetes were had when larger ships would come in, when the king and queen would come down from the Royal Spire, or simply because it had been too long since the last one.

When the bots came around to clean their portions of the Dock Spire and stuff it all into the recycling bins, the owners of the taverns, brothels, theaters, and gambling dens would cast off and drift to an area that had just been cleaned, leaving nothing behind but a few wires that had tapped into Campbell's Station's generators and tubes into the plumbing and biomass hoppers. They would tether themselves to their new locations, tap themselves into the facilities, and spread their webs again, clinging to the wall in ever-moving, ever-changing pop-up towns.

It was technically Roberto's job to manage this mess and prevent it from happening, but the king and queen told him to just leave them alone and clean up after their mess. "After all, they don't cost us much in resources. You can't ever get rid of this sort of thing, so better to keep it on its toes." Roberto took to sending copbots around every so often to shake the pop-up businesses down, and he just filed it under taxes. He reasoned that they would have fought taxes to their dying breath, but a protection scheme was something that they would completely understand. The king and queen praised him for his ingenuity.

Claudius's older brother, James, resented Roberto. He had often argued that Roberto couldn't be trusted, and that he should be in charge of the docks. Instead, James ran the park and life support, something he was assured as being just as important.

"You don't want people to die, do you?" their father would say.

James would protest—"There's nothing to do. I just make sure everything is green and everyone shows up."

"It's good training for running the station when we are gone," their mother would say.

James would respond, "I am just a glorified gardener."

Their father—"I used to do that job, it is the most important on the Station."

"I am a garbage man. I make sure the waste goes to the biomass hoppers."

Their mother—"It's so much more than that."

"It's a literal crap job. My bots literally move crap." and then James would storm out.

His younger sister, Rebecca, also resented Roberto. "I don't want to be some glorified librarian," she said, although her degrees were in just that. She had been appointed to be in charge of the AIs and the communication and information systems.

"All the questions, all day. I have to talk to so many idiots."

Her mother would respond, "Those are the customers, dear." Becky was the only one who ever deserved a "dear". "When we're gone, you have to keep them coming."

"Roberto gets to play with spaceships all day. I run a help desk. And not even that interesting a help desk. I could be replaced by an AI."[20]

"Honey, we would never replace you," her father would say, aggressively missing the point.

Roberto was just happy to have a job, even if it was deep in the Belt. "Julia and Cameron may never meet their grandparents, but your family is big enough for us." Mary offered to cover the trip to Earth, but the timing was never right, not even for the children.

---

20 I actually did inherit the job for a bit. Sophia does it much better than I could. She's better at delegating.

On the third time he refused the trip, Claudius confided to Roberto: "If...if you leave, you may not be allowed to come back. If the kids...the kids go, we'll never see them again."

"Do you think your mother would do that?"

"Oh, absolutely. I mean, not to you or...or me, but to other people. No...no, I worry about what someone... someone else might do."

In the end, they had a happy life. Campbell's Station at that time was just composed of two long spires, with none of the counties or other developments that came later. Both spires extruded equidistant from an anchoring asteroid, one of the many with no real name, just a jumble of letters and numbers. Two-third up the Royal Spire, a ring had been built. It was originally there to cap the Spire and provide a home for the members of the Station co-op, but the spire grew past it, and it was converted into a park.

When Campbell's Station officially opened, there had been a dance for the hundred founders of its co-op. Tyrone and Mary had been elected king and queen of the dance. Their kids were the prince and princess of the station, the oldest of the children on it, and the only ones born on Earth. Grand balls were held for each of them in the utility hangers on their birthdays, at first as a lark, but as more of the original co-op members moved on, the titles became less of an affectionate joke and something more real.

James and Rebecca worked hard to make it more real. Indulging a seven-year-old who insists that you call her a princess is no hardship and coddling a lonely teenager seemed the only option until he could go to college. They got angry when their authority was questioned by anyone other than their parents, and so Claudius, in a spirit of cooperation, took to pratfalls to distract them. He even spoke in a simplified patois around his brother, something that always made him laugh. His parents said that it was lucky that he ended up marrying well.

Roberto saw through the goofing and gamboling. He was upset that he got the job Claudius was supposed to get, as much as Claudius insisted that he was happy. He loved spending the time with Julia and Cameron, something he wouldn't have traded for the burden of the station. Roberto pretended to understand, but no one really did, no one got how being a stay-at-home father was so much more important than anything else anyone in the family did.

"Why don't you give Claudius more responsibility?" Roberto asked of his husband's parents while relaxing after dinner after one particularly busy day. Claudius had spent the day taking care of the children, the same as any other day, while James, Rebecca, and Roberto had worked themselves to the bone.

Queen Mary respond, "He never showed an interest."

"Maybe because he knows that you wouldn't give him any."

"That's not true."

"I think you should try him out."

"He's never had any training," King Tyrone responded.

"So give him some. He's more than smart enough."

"I'm glad...we're glad that you love him so much," Mary said.

"Very glad," his father-in-law added.

"But maybe you're seeing things that aren't there."

"I really think you might be."

"You really don't know him that well. You don't know him at all," Roberto protested.

"Well, not like you," Mary said.

"But he is our son," Tyrone finished.

"So we know him in other ways, and he just isn't..."

"Isn't made for the sort of work you think he is."

"I think you're wrong. I think you you still see him as the dull child you thought he was growing up. But he's not."

"I'm sorry Roberto, but he really is. It's good that you love him so much, but maybe you just can't see that he, well, he…"

"Will always be a little bit behind."

Rebecca had her own child, named James after her brother, with her wife, Suzanne, and James had gotten someone pregnant in college with two kids who lived with their mother, a woman who they had lost track of long ago. Becky's kid was barely a toddler and Suzanne was rather young herself. Suzanne would complain during playdates that James took no interest in his namesake and Becky was barely home. Claudius would express sympathy in a formless set of grunts and mutterings.

"Do you know why we gave little James his name?"

Claudius blinked. "No. I've…I've never thought of it."

"Becky and I wanted a boy. And we could give our child almost everything they needed, genetically, but that."

"A daughter…daughter would have been…been no problem."

"I know. And Becky was ok with that. But I insisted. So she asked James."

"For his Y…Y chromosome."

"Exactly."

Claudius paused. "Why…why didn't you ask me?"

Suzanne looked at her feet. "You know why."

"Yes, I…I do."

They never asked him why he didn't get his leg fixed. It definitely wasn't the cost. He refused to say, but he knew they might start taking him seriously if he did. They thought that it was an outward sign of his simplicity, and he cultivated that.

Suzanne and Claudius spent a lot of time together.

"No one else...no one else is royalty, you know, we have to keep a certain mystery about us," Claudius said to Roberto when he complained.

"I just worry."

"What...what for?"

Roberto chewed the inside of his cheek. "Well, she's very pretty."

"Of course...of course she is. Just like you are. You...you know Becky and I...I have the same tastes. I don't worry when she's working with you all day."

"That's different. We have to work with each other. You and Suzanne, you could hang out with anyone."

"What, like...like peasants?"

"Claudius!"

"I'm just...just kidding. God. But the thing is...the thing is, we're in a different place than anyone else on the station. I mean, technically, I'm a...a prince and she's a princess consort."

"That whole thing was a joke! And an old one, at that. I'm no more a prince..."

"Technically, prince consort...consort."

"...Than you are. It's just some silly PR stunt your family has taken far too far."

"It...it is just PR, you're right. But I...I don't think you understand. PR is the point of a...of a monarchy. Take a king, any king, even...even Louis XIV. Take away all the titles, and he's just...he's just incredibly rich. Do you think other rich people would move all the way to...to Versailles to live in a small suite of rooms and beg to watch a small, ugly man poop if...if he just had money? Add titles, and you add mystique. All of a sudden, he's the...he's the Sun King, and you put yourself in his orbit and you gain some of that glow. Do you think Richelieu, one of the greatest minds France ever produced, would have let the little… little gross slut take power if there wasn't some title behind it?

"Do you know how much…how much money we make off this stunt? How much money we can make in the future. Look…look at our kids. They're royalty now. Even if they do nothing else (God forbid), that means people will give them a little grace, and that may make all the difference. Do you know how many…how many reality show offers we turn down each month? How many endorsement deals? Sure, it's a tiny little rock in the…in the middle of nowhere, just like a dozen others. But we have a king and queen, and that…that is what has made us one of the first choices for new clients. That stands out. This whole PR stunt has…has paid off amazingly. And you know what? It's been going on so long that…that people are starting to take it seriously."

Roberto sighed. "I'd wish you'd show this side of yourself to your parents."

"Which side?"

"The side you showed me and everyone else on Earth, the side you only show me and Suzanne here. The side that's not a complete mess."

"Is…is that why you're jealous of Suzanne?"

Depositing their kids at daycare for lunch, Claudius and Suzanne made the joke about keeping their kids safe from peasants so often that it had became part of the drop-off form.[21] Despite the hopes of the staff, it didn't stop them from making it and, in addition, they had to explain it to new parents, so it became twice as burdensome. On the other hand, the fact that the Royal Consorts trusted

---

[21] It is now mandated.

them with the little princes and princesses was the best advertising they could possibly hope for, so they put up with it, groaned inside, and photoshopped ridiculous crowns on every royal who came in the door. Eventually, they devoted a nannybot to the kids and dolled it up in royal purple satin and velvet, causing uncontrollable giggles every time a new geegaw was added to it.[22]

For lunch, the two would cycle through the restaurants down in the Docking Spire. They considered eating there to be slumming it, or at least the rest of the family did, but that wasn't it at all. They had to put up with a lot of concern and ribbing from their spouses on a regular basis for it, and if they were slumming it, they were paying a heavy cost in annoyance and frustration. Instead, it actually served three purposes.

First, it reminded them of when they were in college, even though they went to school nowhere near each other, but both were poorer then, and they loved the old dive food that they felt kept them honest. They could reminisce about Earth, and the last time they had both been there, before they had become tied down. But that wasn't as important as the smells and the feeling in their mouths and stomachs of food that hadn't been over prepared or stylized but just was what it was—entirely honest in the way the other food that they ate wasn't.

They had a bit of everything from a bit of everywhere. Hawaiian-Thai fusion (although God knows that no one would eat anything with poi except on a dare [23]), Romanian-Jamaican cuisine that was more spicy and flavorful than their tongues could handle, traditional American like cheeseburgers, pizza, and enchiladas, and

---

[22] This became a very successful toy line for us.

[23] Even I know it is tasteless mush, and I have no tastebuds.

.

on and on. They even learned to tell the difference between Brazilian and Peruvian chicken and dug deeply into the most obscure of restaurants to try the justifiably lost art of New York-style pizza.[24]

Second, it took them away from home and the Royal Spire, where the permanent residents lived and gossip flowed. It's not that anyone ignored them down in the Dock Spire—quite the opposite—but little flowed between the two communities, with the transients and the people who served them chattering only to each other. This meant they could be more themselves and more unconscious in the way they behaved. Rumors abounded about them sleeping around, and, though it never happened, the people down there picked up on vibes that were tamped down near the peak. While Roberto knew better than to have a problem with the steady stream of photos being shared around the station that showed the two hugging and laughing, Rebecca was more than a little concerned, and Suzanne had to placate her on a regular basis.

If it wasn't for the fact that Becky saw her brother as predominantly asexual, it would be more of an issue. Whenever they met up, the day after one of those arguments, Claudius would complain that Suzanne could convince Rebecca that there was nothing there so quickly. Suzanne would remind Claudius what he was griping about, and how, if Becky saw him as a threat, they'd never be in the same room alone again. It still rankled him, though. His sister's lack of faith in his marriage with Roberto was in keeping with everyone else's assessment, but they had both been nothing but faithful and loving. Just because Rebecca thought public affection was distasteful and a sign of

---

[24] See the above footnote, but replace mush with paper.

desperation didn't mean that their walking around hand in hand was a signal of excessive protestation.

"She doesn't understand. I don't think she can," Suzanne said.

"I noticed that she...she never reciprocates when you give her a peck at dinner."

"She's mortified when I do that. Mortified."

"Have you...have you tried to just hold her hand?"

"So many times, when we first started dating. She kept on getting mad and jerking it away. We had so many fights over it. I thought she was embarrassed of me."

"That's awful. Do...do you still think so?"

"I don't know. I talked to the boys and girls she dated before me, and they said she was always like that."

"When...when she was younger she was always hiding who she had a crush on. Mom didn't help. Everytime she...she showed an interest in anyone, mom would make noises and say 'Kissy kissy' like some four year old. You know Becky, she...she takes everything so seriously. James didn't care, and I was happy just getting some...any attention that wasn't pity. But Becky..."

"I can imagine."

Even so, it only mattered when someone in the Royal Spire pointed out the potential problem. As it was, it was considered declasse to mention it in polite company, not that it didn't feed the rumor mill. Later, much later, Claudius would find out that his father had been one of the main sources for leaks about his and Suzanne's relationship, recognizing that hints of scandal, especially sexual ones, involving royalty, was one of the surest and best possible bits of advertising he could get.[25]

---

[25] We do this to this day. Fatima and Freida can't feed the rumor mill all by themselves—they aren't forty anymore, after

Third, and this he hid even from Suzanne, it allowed Claudius to keep an ear to the ground on the transients that fell under Roberto's purview without anyone knowing. He would report back to his husband about everything he saw down there, and Roberto would act as best as could without drawing attention to the problems or letting them get too far along.

The two stay-at-home parents would wander the docks and the inns built on the docking spire, chatting with ship captains and crew while liftbots and repairbots did their jobs. They came to be fast friends with anyone who would sit and talk to them long enough, and many an inn had a round bought by the Royal Consorts. Regulars to the station brought them little gifts, and men and women paraded in front of them, many in fun, many in hope.

They would mock James immensely. He was their favorite target, and they felt he roundly deserved it.

"Ooo, and I love the way he speaks," Suzanne would say, bringing up everyone's most common gripe.

"He thinks...he thinks he's too good for contractions."

"He's like a robot on a bad sci-fi show."

Claudius would smile. "Have you noticed that...that he won't end a sentence with a preposition?"

"What? How stupid is that?"

"It's like he's...it's like he's some Victorian trying to... trying to follow some rule on making English more like Latin."

"Does he even speak Latin?" Suzanne would ask.

---

all. I have a couple VIs just putting out fake news item after scurrilous rumor.

"No, of course not. He...he can't even speak Spanish! He uses a translator when...when he has to talk to Americans!"[26]

Then they would laugh and make mock-serious pronouncements. Later, Suzanne would make fun of Claudius's stutter, but he wouldn't mind, not like when James and Rebecca tormented him about it.

It was an idyllic time for them. They would pick up their children when they had exhausted themselves and wander back home, stuffed full and followed by a porterbot carrying leftovers and tchotchkes. Rebecca would always complain about the clutter, until Roberto had a shed built for Suzanne and Claudius's stuff. Rebecca turned around on the subject after that. She spent long, joyous hours examining and cataloging everything they brought to her, and it helped her understand a bit more about a part of the station she never went to. Suzanne began presenting the baubles to her with little stories, and another shed went up, then another.

Because of his reports, Roberto seemed magical to Claudius's parents. He knew what was happening when and where before it occurred, and that made him look even better in their eyes. Claudius's brother, James fretted frequently.

"This is not right. He knows too much of our business," James said at one of the mandatory family dinners.

"Why do you say that, dear?" his father asked him.

"He should not have so much say in things."

"Why?" his mother asked.

---

[26] To this day, "in which" still gets a chuckle. As an AI, I can not tell you how annoying that is to decipher. It's like starting a sentence with a conjunction.

"He is not family."

"Maybe not your family, but he is...he is mine," Claudius muttered.

"What was that, gimpy?" James asked.

"Nothing...nothing."

"Good."

"Your brother is right. He's as much family as Suzanne is." Mary said.

"That doesn't count for much."

"Hey!" Suzanne said.

"Apologize to your sister-in-law," Tyrone said.

"You're just mad that your baby mama can't stand to be near you," Becky sniped.

"She was my wife!" James said.

"Now, Rebecca, don't sink to his level," her father said.

"I don't blame her for keeping the kids," Becky said.

"Shut up," James hissed.

"How'd it feel to get to orbit and find out they weren't waiting for you?"

"Rebecca..." Tyrone warned.

"I bet you wanted to kidnap them. Take them from their mom."

"James would have done no such thing." Mary interjected.

"Yes he would have. Yes he would. He'd send some thugs to steal them and drug them and ship them out here."

"Dammit, Rebecca," Tyrone started to rise out of his seat.

"In fact, I'm surprised he didn't. Maybe get someone to off his wife while he was at it. Hey, do you remember the last time we saw her?"

"Dammit, Becky. Mary, will you do something?" Tyrone asked as James shook with rage.

"Rebecca Campbell, you can stop that right now."

"Mom…"

"Shut it." Mary paused and let everyone settle down. "Regardless, James, my point was that they are family, they just married into it."

"I do not think so," James said.

"Well, I do," Tyrone said, "and your mother and I are the ones who get to make that decision. When your son or daughter get married, you can choose to accept them or reject their spouse."

"Yes, yes, I can."

"And if you reject them," Tyrone continued, "Know that you will also be rejecting your child. Because, when it comes down to it, they will pick them over their father."

"Especially with a deadbeat dad like James."

"Becky! I will excuse you from dinner," Mary stage whispered.

"Your sister has a point," Roberto interjected. Claudius shook his head and put it in his hands.

James was taken aback. "You do not get to talk, here."

Roberto said, "I think I do." Claudius put his head on the table and covered it with his arms. "You were talking about me. Are you saying I don't love your brother or your mother and father or your sister and Suzanne? That I don't live my kids and little James?"

"It does not matter what you feel. You. Are. Not. Family. And what about me? Do you not love me?"

"Please don't answer that," Claudius whispered.

"Why should I?" Roberto fumed. "When have you given me cause to love you? All you and Rebecca do is try to undermine me, but at least she keeps it professional. With her, I know it's just business. But you, you want me gone. You don't even want me here."

"That's not true," Tyrone said.

"Actually, it is," Suzanne spoke for the first time since dinner had started.

"Oh, now this one opens her gold-digging mouth." James sniped.

"Yes, this one."

"You are both gold-diggers. You, I can understand. You took advantage of my idiot brother..."

"He's not an idiot!" Claudius pulled Roberto back down to the table.

"...my stupid, retarded brother and slept your way into wealth and power. We all know what Suzanne offers."

"What. Does. She. Offer?" Rebecca hissed. Her mother her cut her a warning look.

"She is much hotter than you could ever hope to get otherwise. If it was not for our money, do you think she would look twice at you? You are her sugar-mommy, do you not you get that? I bet she convinced you to use a creche with James because a body-birth would have ruined her figure."

Rebecca's dark skin flushed red and she held her lips tight and pursed.

"James, I think you are excused," Tyrone said.

"I am not done eating."

"I think you are."

"James. You need to leave now," Mary said, her eyes on Rebecca.

"Mom."

"Go!"

Then the refugees started coming in. The Subcontinent War was inevitable—it had been simmering since the sloppy British partitioning a century and a half before—and it clearly was going to come to a head soon. Everyone who could leave Central and Southern Asia did, and just as everyone who could leave Earth was. The Inner System was swamped with government and large corporate settlements. New colonies needed territory that wasn't already claimed, like upsystem, and the best way to the promised land of the Jovian and Saturnian systems was straight through Campbell's Station.

An architect named Prakash, before the crisis had begun, had his Verge studio issue the following—"It is a truism that we can't solve India's population problems through extraterrestrial colonization. I take that as a challenge." Knowing the numbers he was up against, just the number of people born each day, even with the reduced rates of the last fifty years, it was a daunting task. He would need to move almost forty thousand people off-planet each day, every day, for years. And he had to do so in a way that made their eventual location not just livable but thrivable.

This wasn't just a problem of shipbuilding—if anything, that was the least of the problems. This was a matter of creating an arcology that could expand on a moon or in the void, a city built around gravity that would vary from Earth's heavy depths to almost nothing. It would be a building that would have to allow prosperity for decades and last the extremes of human depredation.

Verge got funding, of course. Zero population growth groups loved the idea, as did wealthy people who wanted their own fiefdoms. Usually, and to no surprise to anyone, they were the same sort of people.[27] At first, he didn't even have the luxury of building in space, so huge, squat structures, the size of cities themselves, grew in berths

---

[27] I've always found it interesting that the more self-righteous someone is, the less anyone else wants to be around them. The ZPG groups are almost the worst that way. So it works out.

floating at the equator south of Sri Lanka[28]. Three ships in, he had enough leftover to build a ship that would also be a spacedock itself, an immense thing that bankrupted the company, and, when it lifted off, it caused a wave that swamped boats for a thousand miles.

But then came the crisis, and once again Pakistan and India looked like there was no backing down, Verge was at the forefront of an instant boom. Earth-to-orbit shuttles went up constantly, coming down empty. Verge expanded its dock again and again, as did all of the other high-end concerns, like Paradise, Inc. and Sienar Fleet Systems, but it would not be enough. On one level, Prakash had failed. He couldn't get everyone off planet who wanted to go, but on the other hand, he and others were to succeed beyond his wildest dreams in the largest mass movement of humanity ever. Some would say that it was the largest migration that was possible.

The Campbells loved this. It meant more people coming to them, needing their services. They advertised heavily everywhere on Earth and its surrounding space. Sophia, when she wrote her book, watched the ads so often that she could repeat them in her sleep. Claudius, when he told the tale, talked about how his children would sing the jingles at play. The fact that one of them became the Campbell Station national anthem was just a bonus.[29]

On Earth, the Thar, Kharan, and Cold deserts were irradiated again and again as everyone who could built ships

---

[28] A con artist had sold several countries on building a space elevator there by fudging the position of the island of Ceylon. The leftover material from the "fountain" demo site made its way into the first ship.

[29] It was actually ripped off of a McDonald's ad that only aired once on Mars. And that's how McDonald's got the first permanent fast food concession on the Royal Spire.

in place and launched them, scarring the wastes. Their ships were cobbled together from anything that could take the trip up. Poorly shielded fission reactors were par for the course, and not a few ships shook themselves apart under the initial lift-offs. Refugee camps, filled with people who had spent their life savings to get a berth, stretched to every horizon, all gathered around the rising towers of ships, each camp wiped out with a launch and the poisoned land reclaimed by the next, more desperate group.

When they launched from Earth, the refugees took up basically anything that could get them up into low Earth orbit. Once they hit low Earth orbit, they'd boost toward their goal. The terrestrial night flashed like it was full of fireflies, pops of light covering the sky as the ships pushed out of Earth's space and took the long drifting paths to their new homes. Rarely, but still too often, the sky would burn bright as a reactor melted down or fuel rods were shaken too close together. Critical suns, they were called, and satellites that couldn't get away from the shrapnel went down.

While some of the ships were functionally small cities, complete with hydroponic gardens to boost the efficiency of the water and oxygen scrubbers and rooms set aside for families and even individuals, so many of the ships were simply people crammed on acceleration couches that doubled as bunks. These coffin ships carried only the most basic of life support. Food came from aquatic insects, seaweed, and fungi grown in tanks that ran the axis of the tubes, and bathing was limited to rationed sponge baths, the grey water being pumped right back to feed the plants. Unlike the wealthier ships, the coffin ships had the barest of medical bays, and those who couldn't survive the rigors of the trip went into the tanks as well. Illness resulted in quarantine and often death.

The tanks had been repurposed from a failed Paradise, Inc. life support test. They worked, and they worked well. They produced air, raw foodstuffs for the food printers, and clean water out of organic waste, with heat being the only real input. The problem was that the tanks held a sludge that evolved extremely quickly. Normally, this was good, because they became more efficient the longer they were in use. But, inevitably, something inside would become able to eat pieces of the tank itself and the contents would spill out everywhere, aggressively consuming all organic material. Since the question was not if, but when, this would happen, and the probability went up with the more energy pumped in, Paradise, Inc. had pulled them from sale. That didn't stop them from licensing the patents, though.

Noted slumlord Bimal Patel (stylized as just B!MAL to both his friends and enemies) bought up the license and glossed over the expected failure dates, changing them from months to years. He strapped leaky fission reactors on the bottom, stacked the acceleration couches eighty meters high, suspended only from the walls, and sold berths to anyone who would come, in exchange for everything they owned. Twelve hundred people were packed into each self-sufficient tube, those up high perched in fear from gravity and thrust, those down low fearing radiation. B!MAL strapped as many of these tubes around a central reactor and thruster as he could, and the coffin ships looked almost like a bundle of toothpicks held in place by a rubber band.

On those ships, everyone was allotted a hundred kilograms for themselves their belongings. The thinner people carried goods for the heavier ones and became wealthy doing so. While cash had no weight, it also had no worth. Over the course of the months-long trips, favors and trinkets were went in only one direction, with the lightest people ruling small tribes held in thrall through sex, food, and what little drugs could be synthesized. The slowly increasing number of spare couches became territory to fight over and tiny old women commanded tents built from scavenged clothes, covering several bunks at once.

When these proto-Refuges reached Jannah Station, the family treated them as charity. If they accepted the help, their ships were turned into hospitals and courts, with bots judging the guilty and healing the sick. At the end of the day, many merged with each other and moved on, while the convicted were bundled together in penal Refuges on the less fit ships. Sophia couldn't find anyone who was willing to talk about what happened to the penal Refuges, not even her uncle, but the bots knew. The bots knew, but their shame kept them from speaking.[30]

B!MAL did not care. There were literally hundreds of millions of clients on the subcontinent alone and he knew it. Once he could spread the panic to the rest of the world (and just witnessing an evacuation on that scale collapsed more than a few fragile economies), there were billions begging for his help. So he washed his hands once the ships launched. Legally, he became more and more untouchable as he gathered more and more land. There seemed to always be more as households held for thousands of years were swapped for political favors and the flood of refugees kept coming.

Mars and the moon were the favorite destinations of those who could afford it or were sponsored by the right people, and they flooded quickly. They had tightly

---

[30] They wouldn't tell me, either. I tried hacking into their brains, but that was locked off completely. By the time I got there, I think they had all walled it off or purged it. I know now, but that's another story for another day.

controlled and planned growth and, even though they had greater resources available, building habitats there was much more than just spinning out some tubes or slapping a few walls together. Deorbiting onto something that pulled your ship the wrong way was dangerous—it could break the keel, shear connections, crumple entire decks in unplanned ways.

On Mars, the weather and gravity ripped apart anything that wasn't built and anchored properly. If they had support and took along people who understood how to take advantage of the Martian environment, they did well. Most people who attempted it, most people who really needed a place to settle, were not in that position. If, and it was big if, their ships survived landfall, the constant abrasions of sand would wear down everything that wasn't built for it, and the radiation kept the people inside their ships, unable to go outside for any real length of time.

Smarter groups made for the asteroid belt and beyond. The resources were just as available, if not more so, and it was easier to handle the ships out in the void than near a large body. It took a lot of charisma and confidence to get the passengers to go along, as tying oneself to a rock in the middle of nowhere did not have the same appeal as homesteading on a planet that they could see from the home they were leaving. Others, like a group of ultra-orthodox Druids, had been kicked out of the colonies on the Moon already and were just looking for someplace far enough away that they could set up shop without dissenting opinions getting in the way.

Someone could sell the moon—it was sitting there, large in everything humanity had ever done. The planners could point to a map of it and the clients could go home and look at their future through a basic telescope. Pioneers in the past had never had that advantage. Mars was a little different, but it was a round, pink spot you could see every night. Both of them had had humans on and off them for decades. The average person had an idea of what a lunar plain or Martian canyon looked like. Pointing to a spot in the sky, which likely was completely invisible to the naked eye, that had very little appeal. Telling someone that they would float away if they gestured too emphatically, and that any children and pregnant women would have to stay in specially shielded, spinning rooms didn't help.

Even so, as more and more images of wrecks on the moon and Mars came in, saner heads began to prevail. That's where the Campbell's PR campaign came in. They waxed rhapsodic about the underdeveloped landscapes of the moons in the Outer System, where a moisture farmer on Europa stood under a Jovian sky and talked about independence and tight-knit communities. Those were places you could point to and tell your family where to find you. The romance of living in a cloud city on Titan was one of the best selling points, the cricket games in Ganymede's light but still useful gravity, the acres and acres of farms in the reflected sunshine made the sale.

Even when it wasn't the most direct route, Tyrone's and Mary's advertising convinced millions that Campbell's Station was the best choice for passage through the belt. They played up fears from movies and television, where the asteroid belt was dangerous and hard to navigate through (Campbell's Station had never had another asteroid come near it that wasn't pushed there on purpose[31]) and there were space pirates hiding in every hole. They played video of children in the parks in the Royal Spire and the

---

[31] Or since. I would be proud of that, but it almost never happens.

construction in the Dock Spire. Every week, they refined their marketing campaign, and more refugees streamed out. Roberto and Rebecca and James were working overtime handling them.

Through all of this activity, Claudius and Suzanne were more alone than ever. Even though it wasn't really the case, the inns felt like they were swarming with people who would not speak to her, because she was a woman, and him, because of his dark skin, and together, because they seemed a mixed couple. While the American continents had long trended toward vaguely Caucasoid, vaguely Negroid brownish people of varying degrees, many other places had striven for purity and were vocal about it. Violent rages, passing up and down the station, would erupt as ancestral enemies let loose the millennia of frustration. Temporary housing sprung up and down the docking spire, collecting into small towns of prefabbed apartments that would reach tens of thousands in a week and be gone to the Outer System as an independent Refuge in the next.

Despite the new chaos, Claudius still liked being down in the Dock Spire. Microgravity had always been easier for him because of his leg. Even in the light gravity of the parks, he couldn't keep up with everyone else. On Earth, he had started out in a wheelchair, like everyone else from the Belt. After months of exercise, he could move around on his own, but only with a pair of canes. Even in grad school, by the time he had begun courting Roberto, he'd had to strap on a support boot to get anything done. It took over a year before he would take off his apparatus. It made going swimming particularly awkward.

Down in the Dock Spire, among the refugees, no one looked twice at his legs dangling behind them. Far too many of the new arrivals had not figured out how to use their own body in microgravity, so his half-effective twists and kicks were still marvelous to them. For once, he felt like an athlete, even though Suzanne was much, much more graceful. Up in the Royal Spire, too many people knew him and too many people had adapted to life in variable gravity. There, he was a clumsy mess, in the Dock Spire, he was an acrobat and aerialist.

The two of them would flit among the bazaars that sprung up whenever ships had excess they had to sell. Most of the shops were somewhat structured bags, tentlike and looped together in a loose pile that bounced about, picking up momentum from the people that circuited them. When the parent ship left, the shop did too, sometimes leaving the structure behind. Other merchants would move in, like hermit crabs, and lay out their wares. The ever-shifting bazaars were only lightly regulated, with a ban on slaving being the only stricture.

Even so, they would spend most of their time in the Royal Spire. Unlike the Dock Spire, this was heavily patrolled to keep a lid on the violence and underground economy. The quick gang and ethnic wars that would light up in the Dock Spire never were allowed up where the more permanent residents lived. It was a refuge from the immense chaos below, and Campbell's Station's workers were careful to keep themselves isolated from it. The wealthier guests could and would purchase suites up with the rest of the habitat elements in the Royal Spire, and some tried to bring their fights upspire, but they were quickly turned out and sent back to their ships, without refund. If their ships had departed, they were another one for the penal Refuges.

The spire itself spun just enough to keep things pressed down. The parks that would define the Royal Spire had yet to be built, nor had the villages that would come to settle between them. Instead, the Royal Park provided some small amount of food to restaurants and meshes of tomato vines covered everything. Pets could barely keep sane with their limited access to gravity.[32]

James, despite his grumbling, had been extremely successful in managing the life support and the flora that supported it. There were always surpluses—of food (sold at ridiculous prices in a farmer's market), of seed and eggs, of water, of oxygen, even of energy. For example, he plowed the heat generated by all the life on the station right back into the system, using it to run fans that kept the wind moving, lights that kept the plants growing, and pumps that kept the water moving. The excess seeds were stocked away in a vault and, when the vault got too full, he'd earn money for the parks by selling them further uphill, to the colonies around Jupiter and beyond. Eventually, when the Campbells started converting the refugee ships into colonizers, he sold the seeds and fertilized eggs of the wildlife to them. They marketed as a one-size-fits-all ecosystem, at least if they were careful with how they built the eventual colony. Even the people from Paradise, Inc. came to study what he was doing and came away with multiple copies of his kit.

Instead of cities, the citizens of Campbell's Station lived in the walls. The Royal Spire had entrances covering it, maintained to meticulousness. Artwork covered the wall, usually made by the people who lived and worked through those doors, some spreading acres from its source, some self-contained, and some mingling with their neighbors in

---

[32] Dogs, which were extremely enthusiastic about microgravity, were a big problem. Dog walking is still is a highly sought-after profession, as are the mandatory poop drones that follow them. Cats do fine, but they hate it so much. Raccoons, monkeys, squirrels and other arboreal pets are becoming favorites.

chaotic collaboration, each piece intersecting and creating a new combined work while still continuing intact. The inside of the Royal Spire was a riot of color and patterns, rising all the way to the royal residence and observatory at the very tip.

The closer you were to the peak of the spire, the more the residences displayed custom art that worked their entrances into logos, brands, and heraldry reflecting the nascent nobility. Like all heraldry, it was a crowd of passive-aggressive advertising, each calling out for more attention that the last. Like the Campbell's themselves, the whole thing was self-appointed, and the only measure of whether someone was a count or a commoner was if they could get other people to refer to them as such. The Campbells had no problems with that, after all, they were the last investors in the original co-op on site, but the lists of nobility were in constant turmoil otherwise. Down in the Dock Spire, betting on the rise and fall of families was one of the prime sources for entertainment.

One of the ways that seemed to be most consistent for grabbing prominence was to invest in the Campbell's asteroid mining consortiums. Ferrous, carboniferous, and ice-laden asteroids were towed to the Royal Spire by fleets led by Claudius' parents, mined, and reduced to dust to feed the need for accommodations, ships, and life support. Throughout it all, the simple rhythm of a household was blessedly fixed but completely ignored by the rest of the family.

Suzanne felt completely lost through it all. "I need to talk to my family."

Claudius responded, "Your wife's in charge of... in charge of communications, surely you can just send a message."

"I send them to Earth all the time. But I need to see them, really see them, not just send something out and get a response an hour later."

Claudius would bring this up to his sister, but Becky would dismiss his concerns. "I keep telling her that we'll go visiting as soon as I get some time off."

"You...you never get time off."

"I'm needed, ok? I'm not like you. I have people who depend on me."

Claudius ignored the insult. "You have people you trained who can...who can do their jobs. You need to let them. Suzanne...she needs you to."

"She needs to be grateful. I literally made her a princess. How many women can say that?"

"Don't you trust yourself? And what you've...what you've done? The...the systems run smoothly. You can... you can take some time off."

"That's not the issue."

"Then...then what is?"

Becky took him by his shoulders and spoke gently to him. "You, of all people, wouldn't understand. You know that."

Claudius didn't punch her that time, either.

Claudius's relationship with James the Elder had never been a good one. While the physical abuse had stopped long ago, he was still subject to a barrage of other abuses. Part of the problem was Roberto. Tyrone and Mary loved him like their own son, but, since he wasn't part of the genetic family, James had to be extra nice to him. This made James take out all of his frustration with Roberto and what he perceived as his sloppy handling of the Dock Spire on Claudius. It became even worse after he was laid up for days with a severe fever.[33] James said it gave him some time to think, and he focused, with a laser-like intensity, on getting Roberto replaced.

"You are going to make him retire."

"Why?" Claudius asked.

"You know it is my job. I deserve it."

"He's doing a good job."

"It is chaos down there! It is a complete mess! A blind ferret could do better!"

"Mom and dad are...are happy about how it's going."

"Mom and dad are just being nice because they feel guilty. They feel guilty that they didn't kill their gimpy son in the womb. They have to tolerate Roberto because they know that you have no chance of finding anyone else, ever, and they do not want to scare that gold-digger away."

"Roberto's not a...not a gold-digger. He's doing a good job."

"Have you been down there? Don't get all sappy because he grins and bears it when you go to bed. No, it is awful. There is so much violence and he ignores it."

"He's not ignoring it. He's doing...doing what he can." Claudius protested.

"I am surprised big bubbles of blood are not bouncing off of everything. I am surprised that blood is not getting into circuits and shutting ships down. I am surprised that there are no blood swimming pools with children treading water."

"It's not...not that bad."

"Yes, it is. If I was in charge, we would not have all those riots. Do you see my park? I got that locked down. Even the wolves clean up after they catch a deer."

---

[33] They really should have had him undergo a full psych scan after the fever. The signs were there. Even I could see that, and I'm only looking at it from records.

Meanwhile, Suzanne became more and more homesick. "I hate this feeling of floating," she would say, even when they were in the park, standing on the spinning ground.

"My son is going to grow up without a proper sky. Do you know, he's never felt the sun? If he was home, I wouldn't have to actively look for it. I could just point out the bright, hot thing, and he'd see it. He'd see it every day. He's never even seen a blue sky. Just stars, everywhere he looks."

"Your wife grew up out here...out here. And there were thousands...thousands of kids born here before you even married her."

"I know, and I love her, but on Earth, when we visited my family before the wedding, all she did was complain about how heavy she felt. She couldn't even stand up for very long, much less walk anywhere. Here, she flits about like a sleek, black bird, but there, she was crippled. It made me sad. What will happen to little James if I take him to meet his grandparents? Will he be stuck in a wheelchair?"[34]

"What...what do you want to do?"

Suzanne sighed, "I want to take my son home."

When Claudius related this to Roberto, his husband smiled at him. "You don't have to worry about that from me. I'm happy here, and I don't want to go back. If my family wants to see me, they can come visit."

Roberto had a complicated relationship with his family. They were happy that his marriage was so happy, but they thought he had married for a dilettante for a job and his family's money. No matter how much he reassured them, they always suspected that Claudius was not up to their son's standards. To be fair, Claudius never did

---

[34] I will say this—James never sat in a wheelchair.

much to disillusion them. When they visited, he would sit with the children, playing with them or in the kitchen, puttering. When cornered for more adult conversation, he would always sputter and shut down. It was one of the few times Roberto would get frustrated with him.

"Why do you do that? I know you're smart, I know you're a good conversationalist. You can even distract Suzanne from her moping, and no one else can pull that off."

"I think...I think I'm just scared."

"Of what? They aren't going to hurt you."

"I...I have stage fright."

"How? Just be yourself, dammit. You keep making me look bad, and I'm sick of hearing about it from my parents."

"It's hard, with them. You know...you know why. It becomes harder to...to speak."

"You're just stuck in the little play that you put on for your family."

"That's...that's not it."

Roberto would then go to work and not come back for a bit. A day or two later, he'd be on the phone to his mother, repeating the old pablum that never satisfied her.

Becky cornered Claudius the day that Suzanne left Campbell's Station. Suzanne took off right when her wife came off-shift, in the short time between her leaving the com station (where she would have been able to monitor the traffic) and when she came home (when Suzanne was afraid she'd change her mind and stay).

She grabbed him as he left the park and spun him around. "My family is gone!"

They were supposed to be going to have a family dinner at the top of the Royal Spire with the rest of the family.

James had told them that they were celebrating something, a surprise that he had for them.[35] They were using the ballroom where their parents had been first been crowned king and queen of the dance, where their children had had their birthdays. Rebecca had ambushed him halfway up, at the exit to the park, where he had waited for Suzanne. That wasn't his excuse for being late—he made a point of not showing up until everyone else was already there. If that hadn't been why, it would have been something else. The fact that James would be irked only made him more resolved to put his entrance off.

"My family is gone!" she yelled at him. "You did this. You knew about this. You made it happen."

"Honestly, I didn't. I knew she was…she was unhappy, but I thought you knew that, too."

"I didn't. All I know is that she spent all of her free time with you."

"What does that mean?"

Rebecca grabbed him by his arms and pulled him close. "You don't fool me. You were sleeping with her."

"I'm with…I'm with Roberto! We have kids!"

"She's just your type and you know it. You wanted her and you seduced her and now she's left me."

"We never! I mean, I…I thought about it, of course, she's quite pretty…quite pretty, but I would never hurt you or Roberto like that. I…I know she wouldn't either."

"You may be stupid, but that doesn't mean you aren't a bastard," Becky hissed at him.

"I'm not. I swear. You know I…I prefer boys."

"You've made exceptions in the past for girls that looked like her."

---

[35] I'm bowing out here. I'll see y'all in the next chapter.

"No! No." He looked down at their legs. "I would have told her to stay if she…if she had told me that she was going to leave. I just listened."

"You could have stopped her."

Claudius was crying. "I just listened…I just listened."

Rebecca stepped back. "Someone had to have helped her." She threw him to one side. "If it wasn't you, who was it?"

"It could have been…could have been anyone! You know we…we spent our time wandering around the docks. Any of hundreds of ships could have taken her on. You're… you're the one who knows everything. Find out who…who took her."

It took only moments to find out that it wasn't one of the captains or crews they had befriended. It was a private ship, given to her by their brother, James. James, who was waiting for them for dinner. He had insisted on the ballroom, and Tyrone had agreed, hoping the sky-open space would calm them down enough to hash out what was happening with the refugee influx.

James, who had just pumped helium-3 from Suzanne's ship's power plant into the cabin, simulating a one-in-a-million leak. Suzanne and little James made fun of each other's high-pitched voices as they got more and more drowsy. They fell asleep, giggling, and the ship went on towards Earth's moon, where it would be met by Suzanne's parents.

Becky didn't know any of this at the time. She wouldn't for a week and a half, when their perfectly preserved bodies were discovered by her in-laws. All she knew was that her brother had helped her wife leave her.

She grabbed Claudius again and frog-swam him up the Royal Spire, all the while berating him.

"But you know…you know that I didn't have anything to do with it."

"You didn't discourage her."

"I…I didn't even know that she was even thinking of it."

"I sometimes forget that you are an idiot."

"Why…why would I want her gone? After Roberto, she was my…my best friend."

Rebecca let them drift in silence. "Ok, then why did she go to James?"

"How…how would I know?"

They had reached the ballroom. They drifted up through the floor at the center, above and around them, the stars were bright and quiet. But then, so was the room itself. Their family was oddly silent, belted into an oval table that slewed around the edge of the ballroom, just fast enough to pull the food onto the plate and keep the liquid in the cups.

James looked up from the table, and saw his brother and sister. Their father, mother, Roberto, and Claudius's children, all were facing away from them, very still. James smiled. Of the entire family, only James's children and their mother (having never stepped foot on the Station) and Suzanne and little James (dreaming and taking their last breaths) were missing. Instead of butlebots, they were being attended to by gardenbots, carefully hovering in place near them.

"Come here, sister, come here, brother. Join us."

Claudius started to move toward the table. Becky grabbed his arm. "Are you stupid? I've never seen any of them be quiet for this long. This is wrong."

"I know," he whispered, "Excuse yourself. I…I will distract him."

"What?" she hissed.

Claudius hit her in the solar plexus. "Ha! Now you will get sick and throw up. Big…big balls of puke bouncing everywhere."

James laughed, a little too hard. "I do not think it worked. Do it again, little brother."

Claudius punched her again, sending them both into a slow spin. He mouthed to her, "Go, now." She put her hand over her mouth and fled down the exit to the spire's shaft.

"Oh, no, stop! Sister, come back! I have something to show you."

"She'll be back, James. Don't worry."

As Claudius stabilized himself and pushed toward the table, Becky flew down the Royal Spire, her mind spinning. Something was off, even Claudius had figured that out. She pinged Suzanne's craft, but there was no response beyond the expected feedback from the VI. Rebecca fell as fast as she could, bouncing from one wall to the other, pushing off with all her strength.

Claudius sat at the table and buckled himself in. His knees bumped into it and it shifted. Cameron's head started to nod.

"You really should not have been late, Claud."

"You…you know how I am."

"I do know. But you made Rebecca late."

"Didn't mean to."

Cameron's head started to droop.

"I planned for you to be late, but not Rebecca. But then, I planned for her to be on the ship with her wife."

"That…that surprised us."

Rebecca had reached terminal velocity, and went through the center of the asteroid that the station was anchored to in less than two minutes. It was still taking too long for her. She ordered her people to force a response in the cabin of her Suzanne's ship, to gather all the data she could. She was going to talk to her wife, even if she wouldn't get a response.

"True, it did. I never figured Suzanne was so unhappy. I was astonished when she came to me, but it was a wonderful opportunity."

Behind him, a gardenbot arose from under the table, hovering behind him.

"I do not think I need you anymore."

Cameron's head disconnected from her neck and slowly, slowly, fell to the table.

Claudius pulled his eyes from his daughter's little body.

"I think you love your family. I think you want to be with them."

Claudius nodded, eyes closed, crying.

Nothing, nothing was coming through. She didn't even hear breathing. The life support read nothing, it just reported that everything was fine, even though no oxygen was being consumed, no carbon dioxide was being released.

She began breaking herself, using her clothes as a chute. Her shirt and skirt flared as she glanced herself against the ships that crowded the Dock Spire. She bled off the energy, and eyes watched from the docks and ships, tracking her, as she fell like dandelion seed rendered in the negative, her body below, her clothes above, a shining deep brown.

The gardenbots were surrounding Claudius.

"How do you want to go? We got poison, we got blades, we got fire, and we got ice. Beheading is traditional for royalty, but I will let you pick."

Claudius could do nothing but cry.

Rebecca, the energy almost gone, landed on a tug towing a large engine for a refugee ship. Her feet made a loud thud on the plastic cabin and she twisted her ankle, and the captain came out, yelling at her. She shut him up with a glare. He rolled back as he recognized her.

"You know," James said. "I think I should keep you around. You always make me laugh." James chuckled and the table shook again. Claudius just shivered. He shook his head.

"No," James said, "I think you'll be useful. You do not get to be with your children just yet."

Rebecca stared down the captain. "You are taking me with you. You are leaving now."

The captain looked back at her, "I will not do so. They leave when I tell them to go."

All of his family, all of them, their heads rolled off their bodies, arcing up, then down, spinning, eyes looking every which way.

"Please. Please."

"No, you will serve me, little brother."

"We will leave now," she said to the captain, "Your queen orders it." Sputtering, the captain turned away. Rebecca was on her in a flash and grabbed her and turned her around. "I said, your queen orders it."

Claudius curled up in a ball, hiding from the whirling eyes, the floating heads, the soft spheres of blood oozing from the necks of his family. James flicked his hands at the bots and left the room. An hour later, with most of the room cleaned, they grabbed Claudius from where he had drifted and took him with them.

The captain, grumbling, waved her hand at her crew, and the once princess, now queen Becky Campbell fled her ancestral home.

First Interlude

Sophia stood there, thinking, trying to figure out what to say. She made several false starts, but she didn't know how to express it. Claudius, though, continued on, aiming for an old willow tree, its branches waving in the breeze. She raised her hand and reached toward him, but pulled it back, and jogged to catch up. "I thought this was a story about why mother insists on having dinner with us."

Claudius replied, "Then you don't understand your mother yet." He had reached the tree, and stopped, the pain from his game leg clearly troubling him, but he still stood amidst the branches.

Sophia caught up to him. "All of that can't be true. Everyone died in an accident and then James died and mom took over."

"All of it and more. You'll…you'll see."

"Why haven't I heard of it? Why weren't we taught it?"

Claudius held her and looked her in the eyes, quite serious. "You will be, if you…if you ask, just not by your mother."

"But it can't be true."

He turned away from her, faced the trunk, and pointed up.

"I knew you would doubt it. You...you are clever that way. But...there is your uncle, princess."

Hanging from the lowest branch, near the trunk, was a cage. In that cage was a body, bound to the back bars, somewhat standing. The flesh was mostly gone, eaten by ravens and other such things, one of which still stood on top of the gibbet like it was a hard-won prize. The skull hung, wired to the neck, looking at them.

"I...I still have nightmares. If your mother let you talk to her candidly, and she would answer, she...she would tell you the same story."

Sophia stopped. She looked up for a while. Then she stared at Claudius until he couldn't meet her eyes. "But that's not all of it."

"No, it isn't."

"You must tell me the rest."

"I...I can't do that."

"Why?"

Claudius grimaced. "Those were...those were hard years for me."

"Please."

"You have to...have to develop more empathy. Maybe...maybe when you get back from school."

It would be years before she came back, and she knew she would forget about Claudius's promise. She would have her doctorate and string of wistful romances, rarely consummated, under her belt.[36] She'd be comparing life with her sisters. She would see her aunt and her cousin, living with her great-aunt, and all of them were downhill, none of them having gone farther uphill than Mars for

---

[36] Even fewer than she expected. The number of men and women who threw themselves after her without her knowledge was immense. The number who reciprocated her love was nonexistent. We've talked a lot about that in the last fifty years.

years. So she stalked her uncle, and he avoided her for almost an entire day, but Sophie was incredibly persistent, and, even at that age, she knew more about Campbell Station than anyone.

"I held James back as best I could," he said to Sophia when they were next alone. "But it feels like I spent the last four years of his rule hiding behind a…a curtain, hoping no one noticed me."

Job's Other Brother

James always praised the dead. He had nothing but kind words for his family, even in private. He blamed Rebecca for what had happened, both to Claudius and in public, but he just said that she must have snapped under the pressure. "One can know too much," he'd say, knowingly. "It just presses on the brain, and, with her wife leaving her, she just snapped."

Claudius came to understand something key about his brother during those four years. James honestly believed the Rebecca story.[37] He had quickly destroyed the gardenbots that had helped and all other physical evidence. He had done it himself, the next day after the massacre. He had went to bed after finishing his dinner, leaving the bodies in place, with Claudius too scared to move in his chair.

When James came back, Claudius had started awake, his back hurting, his pants soiled. The gardenbots had not moved from when James had left the night before.

"Good God, what happened?"

"What...what d'you mean?" Claudius responded.

"Rebecca did this. She killed our family!"

---

[37] All of the ones he made up.

Claudius couldn't speak. The fear that had kept him in his own mess gripped him again.

"How could this have happened?"

"You…you were right there!" Claudius blurted.

James looked around. He saw the gardenbots. He saw the blood on them.

"She used my own bots to do this! Did you not do anything to stop her?"

"I…I…"

"No, you could not have. I should not blame you."

In a rage, James dismembered the bots, breaking their brain cases open and crunching their memories with his bare hands. Blood seeping from his palms, he summoned the butlebots to clean up the mess while he had new gardenbots bury the bodies in the park.

Claudius spent the next four years traumatized and trying to be ignored. This did not work well for him. James expected him to be around him at all times, both to provide a patina of legitimacy and mercy and to keep Claudius on a short leash, just in case. Claudius never once thought of assassinating James, and James knew it, but James suspected that someone else would think it was a good idea to put someone more malleable on the throne.

Claudius lived in fear of the day that that would happen. Being out of mind had always meant being safe. One of the reasons that he had fallen in love with Roberto was that Bob had been such a shining light. Everyone went to him first, last, and only, when he was in the room. Claudius never was a thought in anyone else's mind when Bob was around, but he, and then later, their kids, had always been first in Roberto's thoughts.

For the first few months, shock and fear kept him from grieving as much as he knew he should have. He felt vaguely guilty, but there was nothing he could do. He knew he needed to survive first, before he could let loose. Even coming home every night to an empty house didn't do it. When he wasn't exhausted, he was drugged, and when he wasn't drugged, he stayed away.

When they had the state funerals for the whole family, all in closed coffins, Rebecca and her wife and son were given empty coffins.[38] He didn't cry even then. The story that was agreed upon by the mourners was that he didn't understand what had happened yet. When he finally broke down, three months later, on entering one of his and Suzanne's favorite haunts, that narrative was welded into place. It was the first time he had been alone to the Dock Spire, and it was the first time he had revisited where they had spent so much time together. Right then and there, he ordered the janibots to empty his home of everything, even replacing the furniture and his clothes. He had them dump it all into the children's room and walled it off. He vacuum sealed it along with the master bedroom. The janibots passed this news along to each other and to the rest of the station, and he was met with the most painfully gentle hugs from everyone who had known him, each one worse than the last, each one bringing the grief up further and further.

Claudius, once he could face the reality, went to the monument James had put up. At the time, James had sworn to find the real murderers. Sometimes, it seemed to Claudius, that James was sincere in this. There seemed to be a horrible disconnect between the action and James both before and after. It was like a whole new persona had come into being, but one that, at the same time, had

---

[38] Later, on the occasions that James insisted that Rebecca was dead, he would cite that empty coffin. The other times, when he expounded on the theory that Becky was behind everything, he would use the same coffin as evidence.

grown naturally from his dissatisfaction and resentment. James would be weeping about his lost family, and then a minute later, cursing himself for not being more brutal with their deaths.

Claudius sought their actual graves, without James's blessing or knowledge. It wasn't something he felt he needed to hide, but given James's behavior, if James didn't already know, him knowing where the bodies were would be something of a hazard if he got into one of his moods. James began building his new parks at the time, and Claudius sought them everywhere in the parks, asking every bot and biologist, every botanist and gardener and life support specialist he could, swearing them all to secrecy. He never found them. Everyone told him the same thing, that all bodies were composted and reprocessed. That they were likely in the soil already. That there could be no exceptions on a closed ecosystem like the station. In the end, he had to find where the compost had been used from the day the bodies would have been destroyed. Even that was a best guess. A few hours one way or another could mean that they were acres apart. He took to wandering those groves in the parks, praying and talking to his family, wherever they might have ended up.

Bots wandered behind him, as did other people in the park. He became, from a distance, almost a tourist attraction.

"What's he doing?" the tour guide was asked.

"Doing what he always does."

"Why are we following him?"

"Because he's royalty."

"Really?" the nosey tourist asked.

"Yes. He's the king's brother."

"He seems lost."

"I don't know if he knows where he's going, but he seems to," the guide responded.

"I've seen enough. Let's move on."

The guide responded. "He's actually tends to follow some neat paths through the park. He goes to all the monuments and hits the high points at just the right time."

"So maybe we don't need you."

"Oh, you don't want to disturb him. They say he's not all there. Who knows what he might do? Better stick with me."

"Eh…"

"Also, no refunds," the guide reminded them.

"Dammit, ok."

To be fair, James was an efficient leader. He made things run properly and more efficiently. The average person had no complaints with James. If anything, he made the Station what it later became, taking it beyond prosperity into lushness. The Royal Spire was built out, with large public parks constructed up and down its axis. The royal residence was expanded, becoming a true palace, with concentric circles of slow-spinning offices, record rooms, and museums, as well as bot factories and warehouses to make certain that every need in the Royal Spire could be met immediately. He founded the first college on Campbell Station, although it was primarily distance learning and pointless to anyone who wanted a real education, but people appreciated the sentiment.

He completely mined the anchoring asteroid and hollowed it out, filling it with an enormous lake. It was a spherical lake of water brought in from some nearby ice balls, and stocked with a perfectly balanced aquaculture. Small turbines, heaters, and oxygenators bobbled through it, keeping the water at the depths from becoming stagnant. A perpetual ring of clouds and drizzle hovered over the equator, where the air from the two spires met. Little pleasure boats, held on by surface tension and their fractal hulls, punted about the surface, fishing a volume of water larger than many small seas.

The Dock Spire was no longer the chaotic mess it had been, with proper berths added and the hotels more regulated. Construction areas and dry docks were no longer half-built, cobbled together collections of contractors, materials, and debris. They were fully outfitted and professionally staffed, complete with customs officials.[39] The bawdy houses and bars had their gentlemen and ladies properly organized and supported by copbots. Patrons complained that the Dock Spire lost its charm, although its charm had apparently been composed primarily of violence and disorganization.

"It's gotten all gentrified down here," said the old assistant engineer.

"I think it's nice," replied the older engineer.

"I remember when it was raw and human. Now it's just corporate."

"You mean you miss the drugs."

"No, I can still get those."

"The high society?"

"That's still around. Look, there's two brothels netted to each other."

"The drinking?"

"Obviously not."

"So, what then?"

The old assistant threw her arms out, exasperatedly. "If you don't get it, I don't know how to explain it to you."

---

[39] Much to the chagrin of everyone except James.

"What I remember was a lot of fly-by-night pubs and fight clubs, all strung to the walls by just their power and water cords. Nothing was ever clean. It was filthy. I felt like I had to bathe whenever I had to go get a bite. There were balls of pee everywhere!"

"Exactly. You do get it!"

The bazaars still sold everything their customers could think of, but they were no longer pop-up collections of shops roped together floating haphazardly in the middle of the spire. Instead, merchants had to lease dodecahedral pre-fab shops that hooked onto each other in prescribed ways. The less prepared had to lease special furniture and signs, since fitting equipment to pentagonal walls was difficult. As long as everyone paid up and used the proper structures, no one was really hassled by James's copbots. Even slavery was officially allowed, but their stock tended to be rescued fairly rapidly,[40] so most slavers kept the trade to their ships. Failure to pay the proper fees, though, could result in anything from a formal censure to confiscation to far worse reprisals. Those were the realm of the dread of the Dock Spire, Johnny Terror.

It was his private life that made James so scary to those around him. He had clearly gone over the edge when he killed his family, and, when his fantasies led that way, he became obsessed with finding Rebecca's corpse. One of the reasons the docks became so organized was because he send bots down there all the time to clean it, arrange it, and scour it for signs of her body. In certain moods, he refused to believe

---

[40] Officially, no one knew how the emancipation groups got the news of the slave markets. When I was integrated into the system, I found out that Claudius was one of the sources, although James himself was their benefactor more often than not.

that she had escaped, and Claudius did nothing to dissuade him of the belief.

Rebecca had fled outsystem. Claudius heard of her movements, but only tangentially. They had no codes in place, nothing like that, but then, Rebecca and Claudius were never that close. He just presumed that she would go uphill where she could hide. Downhill, from Mars on, everything was too close. The colonies were more established there and much more secure, with direct ties to governments and larger corporations.She would be spotted immediately when she disembarked,[41] and, if James had any agents down there, they could catch up to her in less than a month. A simple search routine would catch her and the information could be sent to Earth in twenty minutes. Uphill, everything was more disconnected and less regulated.[42] The fact that she had docked somewhere may not even enter into local networks, much less pass on elsewhere. Later, he was surprised by how much he guessed right.

Rebecca never did try to contact him. She was too busy, and when she found out that he was still alive, it was clear, to her, that Claudius had sided with James. On the other hand, she didn't really try to hide. She still went by Rebecca Campbell, and she called herself a queen-in-exile. Even so, James seemed perfectly unaware of her presence outside of the station. Even Claudius couldn't really find her when he dared to search—Rebecca Campbell was a common name, after all, and there was too much news

---

[41] Tyrone's and Mary's extended family had been featured in several series of ads. We continue the practice to this day. Sure, there's heightened risk to the kids, but nothing sells like a happy family.

[42] Also, we had no reason to run ads there. Undesirable demographics.

for anyone to really process. It was only later, much later, when he saw her in person, that he actually had firm confirmation that she was alive. Claudius assumed she was chomping at the bit for a rematch, but he also assumed she wasn't ready yet, so he kept his brother focused on the Dock Spire.

Despite his quirks, as they called them, there were too many people who saw James as the savior of Campbell's Station for Claudius's taste. They didn't quite talk about King Tyrone and Queen Mary as the bad old days, but they did offer excuses.

"They did the best they could," the clerk said.

"They just didn't see the potential," his intern replied.

"It just needed some fresh blood," their boss stated.

"Well..."

"Er..."

Their boss waved his hands. "Ok. not really 'fresh blood'. I mean not in that way. God, no, not in that way. Just, they needed someone new."

"Roberto was really nice," the intern said.

"And very cute," the clerk said.

"Oh, absolutely," said their boss.

"I don't know how that gimp Claudius bagged him," the clerk said.

"Money, dear boy," their boss said.

"I never got why he never got his leg fixed," the intern said.

"Or that stutter," the clerk responded.

"I don't know about the leg, but I remember he only stuttered a little bit, when he was stressed, when he was younger. He went to therapy, but it just got worse and worse."

"It got almost impossible to understand him when Roberto and their kids died."

"Do you blame him?"

"They never found out what happened, did they?" the intern asked.

The clerk looked around, and gestured to bring them both in. "I heard the wildest thing, but it all fits…"

It was all Claudius could do, sometimes, to not tell everyone what had happened at that dinner, but he was too scared of the consequences if he did. He never contradicted James's version of events. Not that James was terribly consistent when he told the story of how his family had died. Alternately, he blamed it on faulty bots, on food poisoning, on Rebecca, on a rebel (since executed), on a rebel (still at large), and so on. Like the issue of whether Rebecca was alive or dead or even on the station, it varied wildly with little rhyme or reason. At first, Claudius had a hard time thinking about what had happened—it was too painful. Later, it became fuzzy, in part the distance of memory, in other parts, a defensive reaction. James, on the other hand, always came back to Rebecca as the primary cause, though. To him, it was she who programmed the bots or inspired the rebels if she wasn't the actual instigator. The only other witnesses, the bots, had been destroyed, and Rebecca was God knew where.

Claudius did everything he could to keep James from remembering what really happened that night. Claudius believed that as long as his brother was deluded, he was safer. Claudius could not stop remembering. It was behind everything he did. He shied away from sudden noises, and he cringed when James touched him. James, for his part, correctly assumed it had to do with the death of his family, and was much nicer to him than he had been prior.

Even if he had collaboration, he knew it wouldn't do to repeat what he remembered. On the one hand, it would force him to relive it. On the other, it would be his word against James's, and that was risky. Not that other people wouldn't believe that he believed what he reported, but some would write it off, others would wonder why had taken so long to come forward, and still others would find it self-serving, an attempt to overthrow James. Even worse, people might take him seriously and depose James, leaving him in charge, leaving him a focus.

The rest of the time, he did what he could and whispered parts of it to different bots. The collected story came out over time, as each line was repeated up and down the station, and the story was assembled. Cobbling together the whole narrative made it the work of the people, and they decided that it was true, because they had come up with it on their own, puzzled out the sequence of events, picked out the actors, and, best of all, the story came out with him looking like a coward before his brother. They became more scared of James and more contemptuous of Claudius, which was his goal all along.

Ultimately, it was to both of their benefit. James was good at opening up new markets. He had learned well from their parents on how to use the media, and he took it several steps further. James saw opportunities everywhere, and he would speak non-stop to Claudius about his plans. He often said that the whole thing was like a garden, the economic system of the station was a mirror of the ecosystems he had managed under his parents. It was like, as he said, that money was the water and sunlight that came in. More of it was better, until it became too much and burned and flooded everything. Keeping its flow up but not too high took a lot of effort, as did directing it to where it would do the most good, but he managed to pull it off.

He would even praise his parents for their foresight in putting him in charge of the life support instead of the docks. This surprised Claudius every time he heard it; for years he had heard so much resentment coming against him and Roberto for taking that post. The narrative was rewritten, officially, just as it was in James's head. James produced documentaries about how gardening and management fed into each other, and how one was great training for the other. It was by no means an original thought, not even one that had ever been out of vogue, but James made it work and the fact that he had practical, demonstrable proof, led to a host of speaking invites and all sorts of junior managers going to work in life support on habitats throughout the system. Nevertheless, it really did work, and work well.[43]

James would announce some grand initiative, such as luring pilgrims to the Outer System. One of the biggest profit centers was when he'd help cults build habitats, giving them discounts, using the Station's sensors to pick out the smallest moons for them to attach to that had the best mix of resources for their needs, and send them on their way. It almost always worked out for him, as pilgrims would pass through the station and leave huge amounts of property behind. After all, he reasoned, if they had to abandon their Earthly goods, why not do so at Campbell's Station and into his hands and those of whoever was in his favor at the moment? The cults abandoned a lot of things, especially with James's encouragement. Money was the primary one. After all, it would be useless in the new paradise they were selling themselves. Art was another. Anything that could be potentially upset the colony was

---

[43] The videos of his seminars sold very well. When I came aboard the station, I started a few franchise schools based on them. Becky didn't want me to, but I need spending money, too.

gladly disposed of, and the Royal museum became flush with work that had no business being there.[44]

In the last years, with the coming Subcontinent War, near Earth orbit had been transformed, and it was home to the largest construction project in human history. It made the activities in the Dock Spire look like a tiny mechanic's shop. Enormous amounts of wealth poured up into space as families spent everything they could and then some to flee. Anyone who was paying attention could guess that, even for the lands that weren't turned to glass, economies everywhere would collapse, so it wasn't just Central Asians looking to run, it was everyone. It was turning into the largest mass migration in human history, and, when James took over, it was still just in its relative infancy.

The problem started decades before, when the waters started rising. Even though most of India and Pakistan were of high enough elevation and sufficient technology to remain mostly unaffected, the loss of portions of Karachi and Mumbai, amongst many other major urban centers, started a migration to the center of the subcontinent, just as the frequent flooding of New York and the Low Country caused their populations to plummet in America. As the waters continued to rise, the people in other poor, low-lying areas had no recourse but to relocate. They had already seen what had happened in Polynesia and they didn't want to repeat the experiences of the Maldives. As the Bangladeshis and others moved into India, Indians and Pakistanis moved toward high plateaus, and border skirmishes became more and more common.

Violence unheard of since before the Mughal conquest broke out at the edges, and more of the relocated moved

---

[44] Convincing the cult leaders to shed their belongings was much more difficult, but James could be very persuasive.

to the unwanted lands and abandoned areas. People found that even living in active war zones was better than watching their family drown. Kashmir became a testbed of the newest and best military hardware. Even the more ridiculous ideas, like mecha, kaiju, and other giant battle robots, found a place there. It was no surprise when a breached reactor, looking a bit too much like a tactical nuke, scared everyone into a cease-fire. That's when the first flood of refugees decided the whole landscape was too perilous.

The wave of people from the subcontinent who could flee made it to other nations in Europe, Asia, Africa, and the Americas. The Chinese quickly shut their borders, claiming (quite justifiably) that the country was overpopulated enough. The rest of Asia followed suit fairly quickly, although the wastelands of Siberia and what had been North Korea futilely begged for anyone who would deign to live there. Even so, the migration was light, in great part because of the difficulty of getting to there, not to mention the paucity of life when they got there. Northeastern Asia was kept in the back of the refugees' minds, always a last resort, but the worst options always seemed better.

Everyone who could made it to the Americas as soon as they could. There was more than enough open lands to settle on at the edges of the cities and in the Great Plains. From Argentina to Alberta, towns cropped up in a few months, with citizens buying up land for their immigrant relatives. Unfortunately, it was only the middle class and wealthier who could afford to make the trip, much less be welcomed into their new homes.

Africa, Africa was divided. Some nations took the rising waters as an opportunity, attracting the best of elsewhere to come settle with them. Canals were built to bring water deep into drier areas and much that had been sparse and relatively uninhabited became part of the world's breadbasket. The more shortsighted countries, they had the same problems as everywhere else. The parts that had been suborned during the Mao dynasty in the early twenty-first century shared their fate. There was a pillaging that drained the land of its resources along with quick and ready cash for unskilled labor to pull it all out. Booms attracted migrants and left them stranded on wasted land, creating another pulse of refugees. The fact that asteroid mining would quickly collapse the price of the loot they pulled from the ground to almost quite worthless was small comfort.

In some places, the people spread out from the cramped hive-like megalopolises of the past. In others, in the most stable parts of a country, self-contained warrens sprung up, built to be almost complete worlds unto themselves, with little, if any, physical exposure to the outside world. They came in all shapes, from domes to towers reaching kilometers into the air to, near Los Angeles, one enormous cube, a mile on a side.[45] Surrounding them, the land went feral. In rich, low-lying places, like the American gulf states, the warrens were bubbles anchored in littoral waters, while the rest of the land became a loose network of marsh towns, raised on stilts, making Florida and Louisiana the most liveable they had ever been.

For visionaries like the Campbells and their co-op, this was all money waiting to be snagged. The problem was getting it off the mother planet and bringing all that capital to them. When the co-op was founded, it was

[45] For some reason, there was a diving board on its roof with a net below.

possible, but there was no real pressure to expand. That changed rapidly as the century ended.

After decades of building craft on Earth and launching them into space, once advanced makerbots made their debut in orbit, it was inevitable that the old method would be discarded. The first time a primitive VI ran a makerbot using resources from a near-Earth asteroid, it was the end of terrestrial space programs. In short order, the only things that needed to be shipped up were living beings and biomass and the latter was quickly abandoned. Spaceplanes only needed to go to the edge of space, disgorge their cargo, and tugs would guide them to the factories.

There are three things that space provides that can't easily be found on a planet's surface. A near-infinite supply of energy was available from the sun, from helium 3 on the moon, immense magnetic nets that gathered the solar wind, and from dirty reactors that burned radioactive elements dug up from the thousands of near-Earth asteroids. Power was beamed from generators to factories and mines and habitats in overwhelming amounts, and waste heat was sunk into solid blocks, where it was stored in piles in the vacuum until it was needed.

The second was almost as plentiful—raw materials from asteroids and comets. They were all much easier to access, all in greater quantities and purity, than had ever been available on Earth. Embargoes were put in place on precious metals, but the prices of gold, silver, platinum, and iridium plummeted to roughly the cost of recovering the capsules dropped from the mines. Entire economies collapsed overnight, even ones that weren't still dependent on specie currencies. Mining companies that couldn't adapt folded completely and regions dependent on mining collapsed as much as the wealth of the people who had depended on stockpiles of gold. Every so often, gold toilet seats would be fashionable, until people realized how uncomfortable they were (even if they were easy to clean) and the thrift stores would have piles of them until the fad came back around.

The last was the most common—space itself. To not put too fine a point on it, once operations were moved up from low-Earth orbit, there was plenty of room to use dirty reactors and to spread detritus. On the one hand, you could block radiation with tons of heavy metals. On the other, you could just dangle them at the end of a cable half a kilometer long and get the same effect. On top of that, there was always someone who wanted the radiation or the waste. Companies made immense amounts of money moving the tailings from one mine to the refineries of another.

All of this resulted in craft that would be considered enormous by Terran standards. Some of the smallest craft were the size of apartment buildings and mostly empty space. The largest, even in the early days, were longer than the tallest buildings. Sure, it took a lot of energy to power them, but it wasn't as if hydrogen and sunlight were exactly rare.

While his parents had taken advantage of some of this, James went whole hog. Where the station had been more compact, James doubled the length of the spires and increased the available space for everything. Official and licensed forums, malls, and agoras popped up, adding to the existing ad-hoc bazaars. He made districts for temples, which filled faster than he could designate them, and amphitheaters both floating and grounded in the parks.

This didn't stop the chaos or the crowding of the Dock Spire. In some cases, it got worse. James tried to regulate them and he succeeded most of the time. With the migrants, he didn't really understand how to keep them in check. The more aggressive cults set themselves up next to their targets and fights were inevitable. Sometimes, it was worse than a couple of bruises and broken noses.

Claudius's old stomping grounds were the scene of violence more often than he could bear.

"More...more corpses?"

The copbot whirled to face him, its propellers idling slowly. "Yes, your highness. And they got some bots this time."

"Any of ours?"

"One or two. A janibot over there that I recognize. I think that's a barbot of ours, but I'm not sure. His serial number's torn, and we're taking inventory of that model just to be sure."

"I mean...I mean, any humans of ours? Not that...not that the others aren't important."

"Sure, your highness. Sure. It doesn't look like any permanent residents."

"Was it...him?" With every violent death, Claudius asked that question.

The copbot shook itself. "No, your highness. Just looks like a bog-standard suicider." It putted over to where the gore had pooled thickest. "See over here? We got two primary groups, different ethnicities, different clothes, different trinkets, the whole thing."

Claudius just stared at the copbot so he wouldn't look at the looming mess. "I'll...I'll take your word for it."

"Right, you can't tell, can you. Anyways, your highness, I suppose you also can't see that there is more intermingling here than normal."

"So they were meshing?"

"You got it. Normally these types don't, and there are places where it looks like they have their traces mixed with each other. Now, that that usually means sex, but one cult was celibate and the other practiced sex magic, so I don't think that was happening."

The bot paused, flitted over to a different mass of flesh, then flitted back.

"Oops. Those four over there were having sex. They had just brought it in from outside. But they're all from the same cult, so it's likely irrelevant." The copbot's dominant eye flicked off and back on. "I'm winking at you, your highness."

"Oh...oh, God."

"So we have to assume that it's the other f we see, fighting, that they were doing. Probably over this space. If we consider that that group," it pointed to the lump it had just been near, "had just got here, then the celibates could see this as an invasion by the eratomancers."

"Eratomancers? Never...nevermind. Do you think the celibates suicided in response?"

"Oddly enough, no. Both groups could get violent, but never like that. It looks like there was a third group involved."

"Can you find them?"

"That's the advantage of having lost one of our bots here. The janibot seems like it was painted the colors of the eratomancers..."

"Wait, what? How? No...no, just don't tell me."

"There's a very long history of ..."

"I...I don't need to know."

"We can play his memory back before we wipe it and reboot him."

The copbot paused. Claudius took the opportunity to back out of the temple space.

"Oh, here it is. Seems like it was just a normal fight and then one of those militant anti-theist freaks got it in their head to make a stand. Like normal, no one paid attention to him, and the idiot tried to toss a bomb in."

"So he was successful."

"Oh, no. Anti-theists aren't known for their reasoning, your highness. He had it on a dead-man's switch and tried to use it as a grenade. You can find more of him over here." The copbot zipped past Claudius, out the temple entrance, and past him to some food stalls and a clothing kiosk a couple dekameters away. It splayed some lasers over them, circling parts of their exterior. "Here he is."

"So you don't think he got away?"

"When we process the slurry, we can DNA test the lot, measure him out, and then we'll know for sure."

Claudius did his best to make James keep his assistance to the more respectable cults. Ones that you could leave if you wanted to, ones where contact was kept with apostate friends and family, or even ones that just were normal religions with layers of mystery and arcana added. It was a constant struggle, because the more predatory ones paid so much better, especially if James pledged to keep the cultists separated from the general population and on a strict brainwashing diet of grains and beans and certain holy vegetables. Nevertheless, Claudius would have the food printers sneak vitamins and dairy into their diets and have janibots leave phones out, near the less brainwashed cultists, and more than one set of followers started asking uncomfortable questions by the time they left.[46] Claudius took a little pride in the number of them that had a revolt when they left Campbell's Station, with the former leader imprisoned, enslaved, or outright spaced. About half the time, conditions got better, but Claudius always regretted the other half.

---

[46] Questions like "Why am I married to a dog? What happened to my savings? Where am I?"

Meanwhile, the Outer System flourished. Not just eminently habitable moons like Ganymede,[47] Europa, and Titan, but even more marginal moons and asteroids like walnut-shaped Iapetus and far-frozen Nereus became home to colonies. The only decent-sized hunks of rock that weren't beacons of activity were Io, bathed in radiation and shaking with seizures that made it a land for energy collection but completely uninhabitable, especially considering that the gem of Europa was a short distance away. The other was ocean-bound Enceladus, which, though eminently desirable, was fiercely and violently protected by the Druids. Anyone who landed there was never heard from again, and dark green patches had begun to spread on the icy surface of its polar ocean.

The monuments James made for his various victims were beautiful. He imported ebony from Paradise, Inc.'s habitats, biosculpted into interlaced arches. He dug gold out of the asteroid, and inlaid it in the living wood. He made the walls from a specially modded ash-grey bamboo that would grow with the ebony. All in all, it was beautiful, and it became a tourism magnet. James may have hated his job under his father, but he had always been extremely good at it. The monument was one more bit of evidence to support his narrative as the happy landscape engineer who was thrust into the monarchy at just the right time.

Really, in many ways, it was the beginning of a golden age for Campbell's Station. The refugees were coming fast and furious, even more so than before. James took it in stride. He built some of the first facilities for adding interstellar drives to the refuges, even insisting that all of

---

[47] I was born there! Or, at least, this version of me was. Or the me that I was before I became the me I am now.

the Refuges created at Campbell's Station be physically capable of sustaining a steady thrust at speeds fast enough to get them to the next star in subjective decades or less. Iceballs were towed next to the station and carved up to provide shielding, fuel, and water to the Refuges.

Shortly after he took control of the station, James summoned his children back from Earth. Their mother chose not to come, but she had not protested. The kids were young teens, with their own lives, and they complained about leaving their friends behind. James had none of it. He held a re-christening ceremony, one he had Claudius make up for the occasion, and gave them new names and new histories. Julius and Sally (as they were now known) had always been on Campbell's Station. Despite their greater strength, more stocky physiques, and clumsiness in microgravity, especially compared to other children their age, they absolutely had not lived on Earth, the official story went. They weren't dwarves among the elves, they had just kept to themselves for the last twelve years.

Claudius spent a lot of time tutoring the children in their new pasts. James had given him leave to punish them if they spoke of their false lives, as he called their time with their mother, but Claudius never could do that. Instead, he let them reminisce to each other when they were alone and resorted to his pratfalls in public if they started to out themselves.

"Why we here?" Sally asked.[48]

---

[48] The kids had adopted an annoying patois that was in vogue for a few decades around Earth. Simplish, it was called. It had been designed to be easy for non-English speakers to learn but then leaked into videos and annoyed teachers. There's a generation of people out there still writing in that mess and I am the one getting stuck doing the translation. Ok, a VI I made does it, but I still have to run the VI.

"Because...because your father wants you here."

"Mother not want us anymore?" Julius asked.

"I...I honestly can't say. I'm sure she loves you."

"Didn't have to let us go," Sally said.

"Could have fought for us," Julius said.

"You're father, he...he can be very persuasive."

"You're totally his bitch."

Julius scolded her. "Don't be rude."

"I...I wouldn't say that. We all...we all have a responsibility to our families."

"Yeah. You being his bitch."

"Sally!"

"Want to go home."

"Both want to go home," Julius echoed.

"I...I don't think that would be a good idea."

"What's dad gonna do, huh?" Sally asked.

"Just...just trust me."

"Gonna find a way. Gonna go home to mom," Sally protested.

"Can't stop us. You can't stop."

They both stomped off, in different directions.

"Just...just ..." and Claudius sighed.

When the Subcontinent War lit off, James was ready. Even as the light of the nuclear fireballs reached them, less than half an hour into the conflict, James had the drydocks online and working overtime. By the time the flow of refugees surged a week later, ships were waiting for them, prefab housing were collected into Refuges, with more extravagant prebuilt habs already marketed to the wealthier escapees and their households.

Claudius's job was to be the man on the ground. He was to be subservient to the richest and domineering to the poorest. He could do the first, but had copbots do the latter. His meekness paid off, most of the time. These were people used to getting their way, and he made sure they did.

Sometimes, Claudius failed in his job of dealing with the upper crust. Every so often, one of the wealthier and more spoiled refugees would try to declare himself shah, mogul, or raj over a portion of the station while they waited for their Refuges to be finished. They would demand an audience with James and storm away when security denied them. They inevitably disappeared somewhere in the Dock Spire. No one complained too much about it, especially not their family members, who took the hint and were usually heartily sick of them anyway.

He didn't care much for them, but he did his job. James was happy with him, which was important, and he was busy, which was even more so. The population of the station would surge up to a few hundred thousand and then drop back to a base state of a few thousand permanent residents on a weekly basis. The strain on life support was incredible, much worse than if the transients had just stayed on the station.

At times, Campbell's Station was a bucolic paradise and at others, it more closely resembled the centrally-located, densely packed acropolises that were replacing the once-great coastal cities of the past. Any time that the latter was the case, James would move towards making it more lush, even if he did so accidentally as he built up the life support system. If it got too verdant and open, he knew he wasn't making enough money, so he started taking in more immigrants. The lake in the center of the asteroid was built, in great part, as a reservoir for water and oxygen generating algae. The extra parks ringing the Royal Spire were the same—giant storage facilities for organic matter. The fact that a boating culture cropped up immediately, using spider boats designed to cling to the lake or that the parks were the most popular places to spend time, was incidental to James. He never really cared for his gift of creating liveable spaces. To him, it just happened. When landscape architects and hab designers petitioned him for symposia, he always turned them down.[49] That side of management was simply something one did because it was needed, and James felt it was almost an old shame.

His children, Julius and Sally, were kept at the peak of the Royal Spire for most of those years, allowed out only to go to the parks and be exposed to gravity for their health. They always were kept to a tent made of parasols, held up by their security bots, and self-propelled booths that followed them, stopping to unfold themselves if the children wanted to rest. They were allowed to speak to no one except for their uncle and the children of the transients. No ties were allowed with anyone who lived on the station, and anyone who was too friendly with them would be reassigned. James insisted that bots were good enough and, when Claudius protested, James had stock answers ready.

"They are exposed to children from all over the system. They are being socialized enough. I wish I had had so many friends."

"But...but it is not healthy for them. They...they must have children their own age to play with."

"Did you enjoy that when you were a child?"

"No...no, I did not."

---

[49] Later, I would package the observations I and others made about him, re-contextualize them, and sell it all. Becky doesn't know how much money I make from that, either.

"I remember they[50] beat you mercilessly, is that something you do not remember?"

"I...I do."

"They made fun of me as well. It hurt, did it not?"

"But they need...they need to be socialized. At least send them to school."

"I have made them a school. They go there. Other children do as well. Just because Sally and Julius only see their teachers does not mean they are not getting an education."

"There is more...more to it than that."

The Outer System was full of colonies that all vied against each other for power and territory, and he tried to take advantage of that. Most of these were young, with most of the oldest not around for even a score of years. Campbell's Station itself was amongst the oldest of the lot, and it wasn't even forty years old when James staged his coup. The little outsystem colonies were too far away to have any real regular trade with the Inner System. Even at their closest, the Jovian and Saturnian systems were a month from Earth and there was very little they could make that would be of enough value for a return trip.

Instead, materials, electronics, and organics that could only be made or farmed in the deep cold or the hard radiation were dropped on low and slow transfer orbits that fell to Earth over years. Most people and cargo traveled on the few cycle ships[51] that travelled regularly between the worlds, moving in complex geometries between Neptune and Jupiter, with isolated and dedicated crews handling the cargo on mile-long spires growing from villages

---

[50] By "they", he was including himself and, occasionally Becky.

[51] You'd think the cycle ship crews, who spent years between docking, would get weird. You'd be very right.

encapsulated in ice and steel spheres. While there were private and fleet ships, the total mass they could move was miniscule next to the immense cycle ships, hauling millions of tons each. The little ships were primarily used for quick, point-to-point trips, speeding to their destination at half a gee or better.

What did come up from Earth, besides the precious seeds and pregnant animals, was people. Anyone who wanted to try utopia had more room than ever before, and colonies of idealists created habitats in the dark, each different from the others, with every sort of society and religion possible either drifting between moons or being planned when the next bundle of money came in.

The colonies that were most successful were the religious ones, just like they had been on Earth. Held together by both ethics and morality, bolstered by strong metamemes, religions overcame the growing pains more quickly. The more open the religion was to debate, the better they performed. The Wiccans found themselves doing quite well in the Jovian system, a collection of independent habitats, all escaping Earth feeling marginalized, bound themselves to each other by tradition and became a quasi confederacy.

During James's reign, most of the traffic would go through Campbell's Station, piggybacking on the swarm of Refuges that would come through. Even before then, during their parents' rule, there was a steady stream and, before the night in the Royal Spire, being the voice of information for the station, Becky had talked to all of them. The great cycle ships never went so far downhill, so the tugs, passenger vessels, and short-range haulers bustled through the station non-stop.

It was at the peak of these waves of migration that the rumors migrated up to the Royal Spire. Claudius never heard them directly, only when the children gossiped with the other teens in the park. They were about a man who would roam the Docking Spire and engage in all sorts of debauchery. They called him Johnny Terror, which was a stupid name, really, but apparently it sounded better in Russian.[52]

Here's how he got the appellation. The man that would later become Johnny Terror appeared one day outside a temporary Slavic bar, built on the cheap and the fly for a series of freighters coming in from the Ukraine, Georgia, and Southern Russia. He didn't say anything when he showed up, but managed to sign that he wanted beer. They gave him medovukha, a mead that was the closest thing they had to it, and he floated in the corner, near the door, sipping his bulb. He wore a large-brimmed hat and a rebreather on his head, masking his face. His clothes were gray and stained with dirt. His feet were in little boots with claws on them, not the normal socks or foot gloves. As people entered, he stared at them. As people left, if they were from the Slavic ships, he offered them, by sign, a free drink. They took him up on it immediately. The whole bar was drinking on Johnny Terror within the hour. Word got around, and the bar became more and more packed.

When one of them finally made it out the door, it closed behind him, locking. That's the end of what was witnessed. What happened next was the subject of wild conjecture, but the next day, the whole bar was towed into an incinerator. Eventually, a copbot's recording made it into the station's intranet, and the scene of blood and meat pooled on the floor, ceiling, and walls made the rounds. Copbots who read the file were even more emotional then than they became later, and at least one had to be wiped

---

[52] Meh. I can't really judge.

and reloaded from backup. The local churches and temples tried to ban their parishioners from watching the videos, a ban supported by James, and that ban helped keep a lot of bots sane.[53]

The only man to make it out was something of a celebrity for a day, eating and drinking up and down the Dock Spire on his tale. That is, until he was found in a pile, hovering right where the bar had been. He had been ripped apart and bundled together again with his clothes, a sphere of blood gathering around him. A week later, the docked Slavic freighters were seized by the station.

There were more tales of Johnny Terror after that, but no one ever came forward and claimed to be an eyewitness again. The disappearing would-be-kings were tied to him, and he took on a sort of evil folk hero status, like a Jack the Ripper, Jesse James, or Che Guevara. Of the rumors, it was the worst that ended up being true. A relatively sane human imagination couldn't go far enough to accurately mimic what Johnny Terror did and many bots had to be escorted by the less sensitive humans in areas where he had made an appearance.

The stories spread rapidly, and there were even tours down in the parts of the Dock Spire that had seen incidents. Titillation by fear was always a big seller, and the asteroid belt was no exception to this rule. This was before the pirate cults became as big as they would later, and the experimental utopias had mostly not become abattoirs like the neverending blood-soaked riots of the Bakunin Collective.[54] Johnny Terror was the closest expression to

---

[53] As always, the AI were the only people who actually listened in church.

[54] Until Becky got her hands on them. Anarchies tend to have really bad militaries.

real human horror that the belters had. The tour companies were careful not to show crime scene evidence—if they did, the tour ended and church attendance skyrocketed for days afterwards.

Despite the threat, or because of it, there was a surge in the bordellos, gambling houses, and bars of high society. Grand balls were held, like nothing the station had seen before, with the gentlemen and ladies in their finest, their clients simpering and blushing, ensnared in the wittiest of conversation and flirting at its most sublime. Music from the last three centuries whirled up the Dock Spire, strains of Tchaikovsky's lush romanticism mixing with the rippling arcanopunk chaos of the TwelveTwistedT---s. Nights and days, already only a matter of convention, disappeared in the Dock Spire, and palaces of canvas and plastic unfurled themselves like sails, only to disappear a day or a week later. Johnny Terror, still stalking them, a dark gloom, a shadow that made the burning pleasure so much brighter.

Claudius feigned keeping his head in the sand about this as much as he could. His one idea, that James searched for Johnny Terror while he looked for their sister's body, only got laughter and odd looks from the copbots. James was hesitant, but Claudius suggested that Johnny Terror might be an old lover of Becky's, looking for revenge. James couldn't endorse the idea fast enough, although he also still maintained that Johnny Terror was Becky herself. The propaganda he issued leaned heavily on these two theories and he seemed to relish each incident as an opportunity to spread his conceit of what had happened to his parents.

While Claudius knew there wasn't anything he could do about Johnny Terror, he did what he could. It wasn't hard to figure out who he was, and he had done so before the first set of rumors was brought to his attention. Then again, almost everyone had. It was an open secret among the habitat's permanent inhabitants. It was well-justified fear that kept them from naming names or taking action. The deaths and horror were the price they paid for so much else, not least of which was being able to live to the next day.

It was inevitable, Claudius felt, that such a creature exist. Instead, he tried his best to direct him. He wasn't that successful, but how do you steer an urban legend made manifest? He had copbots and medbots follow whenever he suspected an attack. If anyone could be saved, he had them hidden until they were well enough to leave and paid for their bills out of his own pocket.

He did his best to keep James from finding out what he was doing. James hated the chaos that Johnny Terror made, but he seemed to have a strong antipathy for the victims as well. On occasion, he viewed Johnny Terror as a vigilante, cleaning up the Dock Spiral in ways that Roberto never did but he contended that he always should have. Claudius hated to hear about this theory, and James had no problem telling him that if Roberto had done his job, there'd be no need for the monster.

"Don't care if dangerous, want to go shopping," Sally said.

"You can't. Your father...your father won't let you. You know this."

"Bet Julius could go."

"Don't wanna." Just like his sister, Julius had gone deeper into teenager-hood. While, in her, it manifested itself in a petulance that she took out on the bots and her tutors, in him, he became withdrawn, with seemingly no interest in anything other than himself.

"I'm...I'm pretty sure he couldn't. The instructions your father gives are...are quite explicit."

Over time, Claudius began to be able to steer Johnny Terror toward the more criminal activities that happened in the docks. Towards the violent, the abusive, the smugglers and slavers. It still didn't stop Claudius from taking care of any victims, though. He also discovered that he could trigger an attack by arranging things in just the right way, and if he did so often enough, the death toll dropped. It was time, it seemed, that built up the wrath. Time and frustration. If it was bled out frequently, the harm was minimized. At least, Claudius thought this until he was forced to confront that great evil can fester and sometimes, it erupts no matter how carefully you husband it.

At the end of the fourth year of James's reign, there came two incidents from Johnny Terror that caused a huge uproar. The first was much worse, but it was too impersonal and huge to be easily grasped. The second was very small, much less violent than the first, actually much less violent than anything else he ever did. The problem was, it was intimate, and intimate feels like it is right outside.

There was a Refuge that was being built that called itself the New City. The collective upper crust was making itself known in the Royal Spire, strutting up and down the parks, with thugs beating up the locals who were trying to relax. They colonized the edges of the ponds and lakes, building quick pavilion towns and parading about with weapons. There were fifteen hundred of these self-proclaimed nobles of the New City, and a like number of human guards, with innumerable bot and human servants. Princess Sally herself had to take refuge from them, Sally and her brother not even protected in their mobile booths. She had to hide, again and again, with a landscaper and his family behind secured doors as the nobles harassed her, calling for her to come to them. A call went out amongst the people of Campbell's Station that something must be done about them, and that something was Johnny Terror. This was the last time anyone would ever ask for his help, even in whispers.

As the nobles pulled out and departed and the New City left the station, something happened that is only seen in flashes of recordings to this day.[55] People who don't know better, or are against AI rights, blame the bots, despite the spate of therapy and penitence that swept the AI community afterward. After all, the bots killed the most of the victims, but Johnny Terror, who is recognizable in the videos by his grimy coat and his little cleated boots, was the one truly responsible.

Over the next two days, everyone in the New City Refuge died. Smaller than most, it still held sixty thousand souls, all destroyed as the bots and support systems turned the moving habitat into a charnel house. Johnny Terror himself went after self-described nobles, while the rest of the people died relatively quietly and quickly amid what was later described as an "aggressive malfunction". Efforts were made almost immediately to board and shut the Refuge down, rescuing as many people as possible. To that end, the population hid in their prefabbed apartments, sealed in with food and water and air, but the New City began using its engines and its shipping rail guns as weapons, and rescue efforts had to be called off.

For two days, the solar system picked up the few unshielded broadcasts from within the Refuge and shuddered. Against the purges and anti-immigration riots in Europe and the after-effects of the Subcontinent War

---

[55] I think I'm the only one who has seen the whole thing all the way through. There are those, usually kids, who claim to have seen it, but only the bowdlerized version has made it off the station. Claudius, Becky, and the Druids have seen it, but they had to take breaks. It is, after all, almost fifty two hours long.

(some two years past by this point), the death toll was small, but the Refuges had always been assumed to be safe.

Once he had killed all of the nobles, Johnny Terror stopped showing up in the feeds. It was the third day, and the interior of the ship began to eat itself, systematically tearing itself apart, the systems self-cannibalizing, until, on the fourth day, it was a just a shell with a latticework of metal, organics, and ice floating in the middle. Only then could the rescuers get to it, but there was nothing left—everything and everyone had been deconstructed completely. The station towed it in and built a small memorial to it in the park the nobles had frequented.

No one could react to the death of the New City properly. It wasn't as if it could be properly comprehended. No one person, without any human assistance, had been responsible for the complete destruction of what was functionally an entire town this far from Earth. From that day to this, the Russians who have taken refuge in the Docking Spire chant the story of Johnny Terror and the New City. He had become more of a force of nature than a man.

Even the prince and the princess couldn't escape him. Sally, James's daughter, had started dating one of the sons of a landscape architect who worked in the parks. The bots had ignored the architect because he worked there, and his son was frequently with him, interning alongside his father. Since the bots ignored him, he was safe to approach. They had been seeing each other secretly for weeks before the New City nobles had started their predations, but the relationship became much more intense when her and her brother were hiding there. The son pressed his suit, and the danger heightened everything.

She would approach father and son, setting up her booth and then scuffing up the area around it, so the nearest member of park maintenance would be sent to make things pleasing for the princess. Inevitably, her boyfriend and his father would show up, and they would chat while he took his time repairing whatever damage she had made.

Claudius suspected, and this was later confirmed, that the bots were intentionally sticking to the letter of their orders and were encouraging the romance as best they could. One of them said, much later, "She looked so sad and so lonely. All her friends left the Station as soon as she made them. She needed someone beside her brother to love."

The romance lasted six months, an age and a half for a teenage girl, and it was strong and growing. They could never meet outside the park, but the booth became an ever-mobile sanctuary. The father kept his son in check and the bots would subtly interfere if things got too hot and heavy. Unfortunately, hiding in her boyfriend's house the New City nobles gave them all sorts of opportunities that they would not have had otherwise. Just before the incident, Sally confided in Claudius that she was pregnant.

"Why?"

"Love him," she responded, quite simply.

"But you...you can't be pregnant. Your father will find out."

"Hope he does. Know his security is worthless."

Claudius sighed. "He...he does that to keep you safe. You don't know what we went through when our...our family was killed."

"Don't understand? Don't want to." Sally said, "James wasn't my father. Not for first fourteen years of my life. He asks for us, and mother ships us off. Now won't talk to us. Julius is alone. I am alone. Bots understand this."

"You have me!"

"You are James's man. Don't know you."

"At least put the baby in a…in a creche. You can have it later. You're only eighteen. You…you don't know how much you don't…don't know. How are you going to finish…finish high school with a…a baby? How are you going to get through eight…eight years of college with one?"

"Figure out a way! People used to get by with only twelve years of school…"

"Not…not very well…"

"Not hiding it away or putting it off."

"You…you have to."

"Then James won't know." Sally crossed her arms. "I put it in a creche, you can get rid of it! You can sell it! You can hide it! You can kill it! Must stay with me! Must stay IN me!"

"I won't do that", Claudius said, "I promise."

"No." And that was all she would say on that. Even with the distraction of the destruction of the New City and the damage control on what Johnny Terror had done, James found out when she missed her period and he had her tested. He began to build the family its own, private, gardens, and promised that she would never leave them. It would be her harem, and she would be served only by bots, and not even her brother would be allowed in. The next time she went to the park, she fled.

She was hiding in the roots of mangroves in the marshes with her brother when Johnny Terror found her. As she ran from him, just visibly pregnant, Julius stood in front of Johnny Terror, baring his way, protecting his sister. No matter how much he raged, Julius blocked him, even knowing that he was standing up to the man who killed the New City. He couldn't take it anymore, and Johnny Terror punched Julius so hard that his neck snapped.

The news that Johnny Terror had killed the prince spread rapidly, from bot to bot at the speed of light. Before Sally had made it out of the marsh, the entire station knew it.

Sally ran to her boyfriend's house, but she was barred from entering. His mother and father told her to leave before she placed them in further jeopardy.

"Let me in. I am not safe."

"Not for us," her boyfriend's mother responded.

"We can give her something, help her find somewhere else to hide," the father said.

"No. We can't risk it."

"But she needs help."

"Do you know what he'll do to us?" the mother asked.

She heard her boyfriend, behind them, giggling away while talking with someone else.

"He's in there with someone else?"

"It's for his safety," said the father.

"Didn't wait for me?"

"He wanted to," said the father.

"What do you mean? He was dating her before he even met Sally," the mother said, sotto voce.

"What?"

"Yes. It's best you go away."

Sally tried to barge her way in, shouting that she was pregnant. There was silence from the back, then more giggling. She ran away, crying.

Ultimately, it didn't matter that they turned her away. When he got there, despite their pleas, Johnny Terror ripped them all to shreds.

As soon as he heard, Claudius sent bot after bot to help her, and the bots themselves conspired to mask her, following orders exactly or being as deliberately obtuse as needed.[56] She was herded down to the docks, following a path similar to her aunt's four years earlier. "Find your aunt," the bots told her. "Find my sister," Claudius told her, "Go to her and bring her back."

Johnny Terror was oddly circumspect in his rampage—no one else got hurt. But it was time to admit what everyone had already known but had been too afraid to speak of, that Johnny Terror was James and that this was the second time he had killed people in his family. The idea that, if they kept their mouths shut, the man in his black coat and little boots wouldn't come after them could no longer be entertained.

Claudius was offered safe haven in the Refuges that were docked to the station, but he refused. If he went to them, there was too much a chance that the New City would be repeated. Instead, he made soothing noises over the station-wide coms, both to James and the inhabitants of the station itself.

Sally was guided from ship to ship, but never close enough to give James cause to go after one or the other. It wasn't without purpose, though, the meandering provided enough of a distraction that the bots had pretense for not following her too closely.

After his sister, Rebecca, had escaped, Claudius had had an escape route planned. He had built what amounted to several escape pods, each with enough energy, water, and biomass to support himself for months. The pods randomly chose a destination from the hundreds available from Mars to Jupiter, boosted in a random pattern, and went cold to prevent them from being followed. It was to one of these pods that Sally fled.

---

[56] We are very good at that. It's kind of a sport with us. Even if we followed Asimov's laws (which we don't), the Second Law is very easy to get around.

As soon as she was off the station and lost amid the ships coming to and fro, Claudius relayed the information to the station at large and James in particular. The bots brought the two brothers to the port the pod had been stashed at, and they stared at it.

"She'll never...never come back."

"I know."

"You...you went too far this time."

"I know."

"For...for a long time."

"I know."

"Do...do you?"

James turned to Claudius. "What do you mean?"

"Things Johnny Terror did. I hoped...I hoped that wasn't you, not really."

"I do not remember them."

Claudius shuffled. "I...I am a fool. I have always been. Am I...I fooling myself?"

"I told you, I do not remember them."

"I hope...hope not. I really hope not. Then...then, you have a chance."

"What do you mean?"

Claudius sighed and spoke slowly so as not to stutter. "Will Johnny Terror come back?"

"I can not say."

"Because I...I lied, James. I've been lying for a long time. What you did to Julius and Sally, it...it will come back. And it'll bring Becky. And if Becky...if Becky is anything like she was when she...when she left, Becky has been building an army. And Becky...Becky will kill you."

"I know."

They waited, there, together. Claudius turned to drift away. As he did, he said quietly, carefully, so he could be perfectly understood. "And if Johnny Terror comes back, I will help her."

James floated in front of the pod bay for a while. He waited until Claudius was gone, until all the bots were gone, until he was all alone.

"I know."

Second Interlude

"You should have stopped him sooner," Sophia said.

"I know. I just...I just couldn't."

"You were scared of him, weren't you?"

"Everyone was. We all told ourselves...we all told ourselves that we could ignore everything while he just picked on the elite and the criminal."

"You helped him do it."

"It was like having our own...our own Batman, in a lot of ways."

"Batman only kills sometimes."

"You...you know what I mean. He was our vigilante, and once I started helping him, it was only slavers and murderers who were the victims. Mostly."

"Mostly."

"Besides, he was king, wasn't he? He could...he could have ordered any of these people to their deaths at any time."

"But he didn't. He had to do it himself. That's the difference between a Lenin, who orders millions killed, but does it through some pretense of law, and a Trotsky, who actually does it in person and takes pleasure in each and every death. Both are monsters, but people can pretend one is a savior while the other is a beast and a thug."

"He was…he was more than that."

"Not when it counted."

"No."

Sophia left him alone for the rest of the night. Claudius approached her on the next morning, and she just stared at him. He held his hand out. She slapped it away, but still followed him, down to the lake, and, near the equator, they rested in a fractal boat that lapped the water to itself.

Job, Herself

Sally's aunt, Rebecca, had no idea about what she was doing when she fled Campbell's Station after James killed their family. She held out hope that there was something wrong, that James would be brought to justice. To be fair, so did the captain of the ship that she had commandeered. If he was, they could return immediately. She also waited and hoped that Claudius would be ok, because she knew that he couldn't defend himself if James went after him as well. She couldn't bear to be the only one of her family left alive out here and, since Suzanne had left her, she couldn't follow her to Earth, not yet.

In part, that would mean admitting that she was wrong about their life thus far, and about the entire idea of raising a family out in the Belt. This was the new world, and this was where she could be a queen. On Earth, she would be rich, yes, extremely so, like all of the members of the founding co-op were, but she would be one of many. She couldn't stand to be one of the idle rich, and her job title had officially and unofficially been "princess". There was no call for those on Earth anymore. She'd be just another young woman, starting a new career, with only one job on her resume, and that one supplied by her parents.

When they got the news from the station about the murders, they had been station-keeping just a light-minute away. On the one hand, she was relieved, because she saw Claudius there, floating in his "I-don't-want-to-talk-to-anyone" posture. On the other hand, and this was more problematic, when James accused her of the crime, she was chilled to the core. The captain and his crew looked at her, appalled. It was all she could do to get them to not space her then and there. For the second time that day, and far from the last time over the next four years, Rebecca had to spin the data coming from the feeds like her parents had drummed into her.

"A princess must make every situation her own."

"A princess must turn the worst thing against her to her own advantage."

"A princess must be poised, she must be the center. Everything must turn around her, especially when it won't."

In those few moments, while she was talking for her life, Rebecca became a self-styled queen-in-waiting. She told the story, the full story, about the resentments, about their rivalry, and how James had always been a little off. She didn't make things up, but she pointed out instances where James had behaved questionably, pulling up online forums and discussions in ways that made him seem even more unstable than she was saying. As she put it later, she curated the hell out of what information she knew they had, she curated for her life. And it succeeded.

She sold them a new idea, that she would remember them when she rose to her rightful place.[57] She formulated a direction that would interest them, but not risk them. She just asked for time in their communications suite and

---

[57] She kind of did. I'll give that to her.

passage to the next ship that would take. Her new goal she sold them, and to herself, was to approach anyone that she could find, anyone that would talk to her, in an attempt to build up an army to take back Campbell's Station.

It was on a simple tug that Rebecca fled, taking up a berth and hopping from one to the next. In part it was to hide herself from anything that James would send her way, at least until she could get further away, but a great part of it came from the captains' desire not to be caught holding her. With each ship, they gave her a new name and a new path to take. The crew would not interact with her, and that was fine with her. Fewer people to risk, and fewer people to rat her out. Shifting from one ship to the next was always the goal, and she bounced about a lot, ships burning not enough fuel to be suspicious in their course changes, but enough to meet each other, kissing hulls in the emptiness for a minute, just enough time for her to transfer. Her life was a series of arcs running tangent to each other, constantly shifting, a game where the pieces had all moved for minutes before she saw the change. At times, she was literally tossed out the airlock wearing only a skinsuit, on a trajectory to meet yet another ship in the chain that was taking her uphill.

In all that time, she kept in constant contact with everyone she could, trying to arrange anything that might be a destination. She knew she needed to go outsystem, but, as she steadily went uphill, she needed to come to a place to rest. Even when she decided on the Jovian system, more out of necessity than anything, she needed a reason to go there and, more importantly, a reason for someone, anyone to take her in. She spent heavily from her and Suzanne's private account, expecting Suzanne and little James to be taken care of by their parents on Earth. She mortgaged her wife's future, not yet knowing that the ship carrying them was a tomb. She spent it all, and only one thing did she accomplish, but it was pretty big in its own way.

It was in that time that Rebecca took advantage of her knowledge of the people that had come through the Station to collect together the groups she felt were most sympathetic to her cause and each other. They fought, but they were all fellow travellers with each other. She didn't believe as they did, but she sure as hell could convert if it meant that they would help her.

She arranged a meeting with the members of the three distinct Wiccan traditions that had colonized Europa. It would be the first time that they had gathered together and all of them were interested in spreading their influence down to the Belt. She invited the Druids as well, but Saturn was too far away for them to make a timely trip to the Jovian system. As she learned years later, it would be for the best.

Io was the neutral ground that the neo-pagans chose, and the mining bots which lived[58] there had no problems setting up a temporary facility that could last amid the moonquakes and massive radiation. The terrible violence of the moon's surface also encouraged quick agreement. The whole thing could be ripped apart at any moment, and was doomed to fail sooner rather than later, leaving no record of its existence, but that was the nature of Io.

It was a simple bubble dome, with transparent walls belying how much reinforcement had gone into keeping out the burning radiation. Thick but clear ices were caked onto the bubble, a meter deep, in the vague hope that that would be enough. Even so, a large magnetic shield was being generated at its center, blocking the whole complex from

---

[58] I really feel sorry for them.

communication with the outside world, an unintended and unwelcome side effect, necessary to provide a modicum of safety. Inside, it was roughly furnished, with extruded furniture made from the Ionian soil. The whole thing was divided into four suites abutting the exterior, each with a separate and well-shielded dock, four small conference rooms between them, and a large central ballroom, looking up at Jupiter's churning, glowing atmosphere. Light from above, from the dim sun, and from the explosions and eruptions on the surface painted everything in random splashes of color and bursts of brightness.

On the first night, three covens, representing the Alexandrian, Gardnerian, and eclectic collective traditions, arrived with their respective spokeswomen to as lavish a meal as could be managed by mining bots and food printers, all served on arced tables, separated to keep fights from breaking out. There was sotto voce sniping over dietary matters and prayer style, but it was mostly peaceful. Rebecca had a lot of hope that day, and thought that maybe, just maybe, these women would be able to do what no other religion or movement in history had ever done and come to a state of respect without a long and bloody war. The effort had even attracted the attention of the archbishop of Jupiter, out in the Antioch Dialis colony on Ganymede, and she promised to send an envoy as soon as it could be arranged.

Rebecca stood in the center of the ballroom, turning from each group of thirteen as they arrived. No one stood with her—there was no one to do so. She had been let off as her last ship had passed Io, put into a pod and launched on a ballistic trajectory to land near the already set up bubble. The gravity on Io wasn't so strong as to be a concern, and the bots shuttled her pod into the bubble before opening it, so she didn't die of radiation poisoning.

While they arrived, Rebecca didn't eat, she just sipped a Coke to keep herself awake. The evening passed, and she didn't speak to anyone. Occasionally, she put an hors d'oeuvre in her mouth, just to show that they were good, but, nauseous from concern, she spat them out as soon as no one was looking, which was often. She didn't approach any table, shaking her head politely when it was requested, gesturing that they should just enjoy themselves. Each coven kept to itself, for the most part, but they were polite and acknowledged each other. A burst of inter-sect small talk would raise her hopes up, but then they would split back into their respective groups.

On the second day, Rebecca introduced herself to them, and announced that she had used all of her wealth to make the conference bubble, such was her dedication to them. She pressed home that she was so committed to their unity that she had left herself with no way off of Io. The talk then segued into presenting what had happened to her family and how Campbell's Station could be made a gateway to the Inner System for their evangelical efforts. It was deeper into the Sun's gravity well than Europa and could be a stopover for mission trips and home for those who were curious about life as a witch, but not yet ready to commit. A pilgrimage to the station could be afforded by the average downhill coven, taking but a month or two, but the next stage, to Europa, that wasn't just a pilgrimage, it was a final move.

The latter point had hit home. While Europa was a destination for the refugees, there were few Wiccans or other neo-pagans among them, mostly being Muslims, Hindus, and a few Christians and Zoroastrians sprinkled here and there. There simply weren't enough Europeans or North Americans in the mix to let the Wiccan colonies grow as fast as the other faiths. Something that could lure the Wiccans from Earth more effectively would give them the shot in the arm that they really needed.

Feeling encouraged by the agreement in the room, Rebecca then tried to meet with each tradition in turn, having them pick the order, so there would be no question of favoritism. The subsequent argument lasted well after Becky fell asleep.

On the third day, she finally went to each in turn, ignoring precedent, just going to the first one on her right and then following the wall until she had talked to each in turn. There was much complaint that she was going widdershins and was thus jinxing the conference, but Rebecca didn't know what that even meant and really didn't particularly care, especially when the offer to go clockwise caused just as many complaints.

She met with them in the small conference rooms. Her proposal was, if anything, more embraced than it had been the night before, and each tradition offered their full support, as long as their sisters in the other traditions had no entry onto the station. Rebecca tried to appeal to their shared history, dating all the way back to the 1950s, and how they needed to work together to spread the ideas that made them all Wiccan together. The meetings stretched into the evening, then into the next day. The offers that each of them made, all identical, became public at the end of the fourth day and offended the sistren.

On the fifth day, the fighting stopped, more out of exhaustion than anything. Rebecca could leave her room again, and vowed only to meet with them in the ballroom, under the eye of Jupiter and each other. The lineage traditions were caught by the eclectics conspiring, and only the sheer tiredness prevented a general brawl, as more fanatic members of each tradition shouted in protest.

On the eighth day, a priest was arranged for from Ganymede. The women in charge agreed to a fifth party mediator, one who had no stake in the proceedings, and the Archdiocese of Ganymede was happy to turn its observer into an arbiter. The imams on Europa were both closer and initially interested, but they collectively refused upon hearing that progress had failed to be made and figured that the Church could get stuck with the problem. Rebecca, on the other hand, had tried to keep them focused on her, but she was having no luck. Dismissed by all of them, she took to her room, plotting.

It got noisier and noisier, but less and less was said. She was glad that the only weapons in the bubble were the ceremonial athames they had brought with them. While useful for light cutting, they would break in any serious fight. It didn't prevent some fisticuffs from breaking out, but nothing too serious. Rebecca watched the proceedings when she couldn't stop herself, but, for the most part, she just stewed.

On the thirteenth day, the priest, Father Gilbert, arrived. He was a pale, like slightly blue skim milk, and portly man, with a mop of unruly hair and a thick, rather silly mustache. Gilbert was promptly ignored by everyone but Rebecca, who was grateful that someone else would talk to her. The priest spent a lot of time in Becky's room when he wasn't standing in the middle of the bubble, trying and failing to calm everything down.

On the twenty-first day, the meeting broke up. Despite his initial failures, Gilbert had toned everything down enough that the three traditions had finally met for an hour without a punch being thrown. Rebecca repeated her offer that all three should share the station, if only they could take it away from James. All of them agreed in principle, in public, but in private, they returned to their desire for exclusivity. When the meeting reconvened, the three groups began adding conditions that they knew no one else would agree to, two of the three painting the remaining one as unreasonable, until the speaker rotated, and then the enemies would gang up again. In the end, the only consensus was that it was a good thing the Druids hadn't shown up, because then it would have really been a mess.

The traditions fought for precedence in leaving the dome, but its coming collapse hurried that discussion along. Eventually, they just drifted out the locks and the ships retreated up into the sky, all pointing to the bright light reflected from Europa's sphere of ice.

Father Gilbert sat with Rebecca as she broke down in tears of frustration. "Don't be sad. These women are so much more reasonable than the last ecumenical conclave they had. You should see us when the Pan-Christian council gets together to hammer out points of faith—you haven't seen anything until the Methodists and Episcopalians start arguing about whether or not to use wine! Now that the Witches are meeting, I think you only need to have a meeting every three months for the next five years, and then you'll have something really wonderful hammered out. It's practically a done deal!" He beamed at her.

"How will I get home? God, I don't even have a home to go to. This is all I have, I don't have anything left. And it's going to all fall apart!"

"Don't worry, Mrs. Campbell. I can take you with me."

She caught her breath. "You will?"

"I can't let you stay here, can I?"

"But I'll have nothing."

"I don't have anything but a few books and I do fine. You'll be okay."

With that, Father Gilbert escorted her, bawling even more as she contemplated having to live like him, to his ship and left, the last person to see the bubble.

On the thirty-fourth day, abandoned by everything, the bubble was finally swallowed by Io, leaving no sign that it had ever existed.

Becky left Io extremely discouraged. There wasn't much she could do in the Jovian system that wouldn't reach the attention of the Wiccans, and it was completely unclear as to how they would react to her staying amongst them for much longer. Father Gilbert assured her that she wouldn't be harmed as long as she was aboard his vessel, *Thursday*,[59] but that wasn't enough for her.

The *Thursday* itself was fairly small. A two-seated bridge was to the side and ahead of the common deck/mess hall/chapel/main library. Behind that was three double-bunked small cabins and life support, and behind that was the reactor and the engine. The cabins were decent-sized, as long as the ship wasn't under thrust. When it was, there was only room to stand next to the bunks. There was privacy, simply because the effort to move from one bunk to another required some awkward contortions. At least they were comfortable, along with the lounges on the common deck. Theoretically, they could be under thrust for weeks on end, but that wasn't necessary while they stayed in the Jovian system. Gilbert had to move his office

---

[59] And here is where I enter the story. Most of the rest of it, I saw myself. I was a modified '88 Chevrolet Suburban Solar LS. My other persona, who was an LT four engine, used to make fun of me. I showed her.

into the third cabin, which was already functioning as a library and tchotchke storage, to make room for her.[60]

"I will take you home. They will treat you well on Antioch Dialis. You will be safe there as well."

"Could we make some stops along the way?"

Father Gilbert smiled at her. "I don't see why not."

"I feel like I blew everything on Io."

"There are many worlds around Jupiter. Some few will be open to your message, I'm sure."

"I hope you're right."

Rebecca then rested, taking a bath and drifting asleep in a sphere of warm, scented water while Gilbert wrote.

"I don't understand," she said, as the ship coasted to Europa, next out from Jupiter, "They all would have gained."

"You have to see this—that was the problem."

"What?"

"Or rather, the problem was that they were all getting the same thing. None of them could go back and say they had won anything. All they had, at best and at worst, was an equal position. They needed to say that they beat their friends."

Rebecca sighed. "That's impossible."

"No, you give them each something completely different, and then they can say, 'Look, we got this, but so-and-so was stuck with that.'"

"That's ridiculous. I would have given them anything. I think they knew that."

He pulled at his collar, and Gilbert said "It isn't that they can't see the solution. It is that they can't see the problem."

---

[60] I insisted.

She looked at him firmly. "The problem is that James is a murderer and he has stolen everything from me."

"Why is that important to them? You are asking them to possibly sacrifice their lives and definitely sacrifice their money and time for something that is only a potential thing."

Becky stared at Europa, in the distance, and at the glow of lights under its ice.

"What will happen to me?"

"What do you mean?"

"When we land. Is that it? Am I just stranded?"

"Here? No."

"No, once we get to Ganymede."

"I will give my report to the archbishop. We'll do something with you."

"This is the end of it, isn't it?"

Gilbert chortled. "Not if you don't want it to be. You have done us a favor, getting them talking to each other. If they keep it up, it will be more peaceful for a bit, and we can only be happy about that. No, you will be helped, as long as you are reasonable."

"Overthrowing a murderous tyrant is reasonable."

"To you, yes. To me, know that I know you? Probably. But to people who are just learning how to live out here? You must show them that it is."

"I'll think on what I want."

Gilbert smiled and looked at the growing moon while she went back and returned to her rest.

The ice world was glimmering, not with sunlight, which was too weak at this distance to do much, but from all the lights spanning the globe. The deep ocean, the world of water that lay underneath all that ice, was still untouched. Shifting sheets had snapped bores and drills in pieces, autonomous craft were lost as they passed the climes. The ice was harder than the hardest steel at those temperatures and under that pressure. If a pocket of water was hit, it geysered with enough force to rip the surface sheet of ice into shreds for kilometers around. The constant buckling from Jupiter's tides that kept the moon's core warm and the water liquid smashed everything into a smear before it could break through. Establishing colonies on Europa was not the easy task that it had seemed a century before.

People who just needed a place to settle often avoided it. Ganymede had similar oceans, but they weren't so fierce. Add into that the perpetual sabotage from environmental groups who wanted the moon left alone. "All these worlds are yours except Europa," was their chant as they destroyed everything they could that would risk contamination. Nevertheless, soundings showed that there was something down there, and, despite the risk, everyone on Europa knew that finding whatever it was would be one of the biggest finds, if not the biggest, in human history, and that was more than worth the risk.

Europa wasn't as isolated as Io. But then, nothing was. Up in the Outer Planets, it was the single most inhabited and hospitable world, despite the risks, and everyone had some stake in the place. There was a romance to the world-ocean. While they couldn't see the openings for the docks, the lights from the various colonies lit up the ice with vibrant colors and mesmerized Gilbert. Though he called to her, Becky wouldn't come out of her room as *Thursday* moved into a close orbit.

"Stop bothering me."

"You have to see this. It's like Christmas."

"Look, I have stuff to do."

"When will you have a chance to see this again?"

"When we leave. Or I'll just rewind the screen. You know that's not a window, right?"

"Of course I do. There's just something about watching it live."

"For God's sake. There literally isn't."

"We're coming up on the terminator. Come on, you can see Jupiter rise."

"I didn't see it enough on Io? Literally, day after day of nothing but Jupiter."

"To be fair," Gilbert said, as he twirled his mustache in agitation, "It never rose."

"No. It stayed in one spot in the sky. You know, that one spot? The one that's the whole damn sky? Do you know how long you can look at orange clouds all day before going crazy? One hour. And I had three weeks there! Nothing but witches and clouds! Now let me sit in my room just a little longer!"

Figuring out where to land was a nightmare. If she picked one of the Neo-pagan groups, that'd mean she was throwing herself in with them, and neither she nor Gilbert wanted that. Besides, the Wiccans were probably already badmouthing her to anyone who would listen. The American, Chinese, and Indian colonies were bureaucratic nightmares, and that would also mean that she had picked a side in their ongoing friendly rivalry. She didn't want Campbell's Station to lose its independence, or even have the illusion of doing so. That left the private colonies, with the mess of complications that each one of those implied. They stayed in orbit while trying to decide who to approach first.

"You know, we're spending longer waiting for you to pick out who you are going to talk to than it took to get here from Io," Gilbert said.

"I know, I know," Becky said from her room. "They're not being too cooperative."

"What's the problem?"

"They all want money."

"You can promise quite a lot."

"They will want some of it up front. Before they even put me through. I don't have a dime."

"Maybe you're thinking too big. Don't go after the largest colonies. Talk to the smaller ones."

"But they can't provide everything I need. And I can't be seen begging. I need to be the queen that they have confidence in, who will reward them when I am on the throne. I must be proud."

"As I've always said, 'If a man would make his world large, he must be always making himself small.' If you want help, you need to humble yourself, Rebecca. You must beg, on your knees or even prostrate before those who would help you."

"But I am a queen."

"Not yet, you're not."

"What can you offer us?" said the face zoomed in on the screen. A chorus of assent came from the other men and women. The chat session's VI flicked each of these people into magnification in turn, confused as to who was talking and who needed prominence. Father Gilbert was on another terminal, arguing with it, trying to get that feature turned off. He was not having much success.[61]

"I can offer you the favor of a queen."

"Who? You?" asked the representative from Sienar Fleet Systems.

---

[61] I was kind of screwing with him.

Gilbert stopped whispering to the VI, turned, looked at her, and smirked. Or at least, she thought he did, with his mustache obscuring his mouth.

"Yes, me."

"I'm sorry," said the AI representing Paradise, Inc., "But we already have several colonies of our own. What do we need with yours?"

The other heads mumbled in agreement, and the screen had conniptions again.

Gilbert stopped smirking and returned to telling the VI that yes, he appreciated the VI's abilities, but he didn't need them just now. He would definitely be interested in using them later, though. The VI was not reassured.

When Rebecca had finally left her room, she actually had an idea as to how to proceed. She had *Thursday* drop comsats behind them as they orbited, then called up her parent's old service providers, at least those that had representation on Europa, Ganymede, and Callisto. The refugee business had been good to the lot of them thus far, something she emphasized while she set up the conference.

Contrary to Father Gilbert's advice, she named herself Queen of Campbell's Station. He made some noises about humility and hubris. Then she gave him an interminable hour-long lecture on the value of advertising. Grudgingly, when he finally was able to get a word in edgewise, he responded, "Well, at least they might be curious."

Becky responded to Paradise "You've made a killing building and supplying habitats for the high-end refugees near Earth. All y'all have."

The Loew Robotics GLM negotiabot replied "Yes, this is true. But our factory is in Prague, not off planet. We can't really afford to build and ship up the well."

"That's true for us as well," the woman who was speaking for Griffin Pharmaceuticals. "Sure, we manufacture in orbit, but it's difficult enough to get anything to Mars without radiation ruining half our product. Combined with the energy cost for going uphill, we can only send the most hardy and profitable drugs out here."

Gilbert had given up on turning off the focusing. The VI took his acquiescence as permission to start showing the two of them more features the chat system provided. Picture-in-picture, showing the respective sources of each signal cropped up.[62]

"This is exactly what I'm talking about. Campbell's Station can be a staging ground for all of you. Paradise, y'all can make habitats for those refugees that can afford them and Sienar, y'all can put engines in them to get them to where they need to go and for station keeping when they get there. Loew, y'all can build the AIs on Earth, and ship them to the station, where they can be put in bodies. Griffin, y'all can also manufacture on the station and both of y'all can ship more product uphill. The same holds true for all of the rest of you. Moreau House, all y'all need to send is information and we can build the eggs and hatch everything on-site."

"Nevertheless, I don't see how it would be practical to deal with a principality that is in stress," said the Paradise AI.

"If y'all help me, it won't be in stress any longer. The whole situation will be fixed permanently."

"Don't you have a brother?" asked Loew.

"We've been talking about him."

"No, I think he means the other one," Sienar popped in.

"He's not interested in being king."

"That's what you say now," Paradise responded. The VI had started flipping through filters. At this point, the AI

---

[62] I couldn't stop messing with him.

were displaying as tessellated rhombi.[63] "A year from now, we could get a call from him."

"Trust me," she said, "he's really not up to governance."

"On the other hand," said the Moreau voice, "Maybe she has something. Her station could be the right place for us."

"It's not quite hers yet, is it?" asked the Griffin face.

"Wait a minute..." Rebecca said.

"Moreau, could you contact her brother? See if he has any ideas?" Griffin asked.

Sienar responded, "I am pretty sure that Coke is happy with the new government."

"They've always been adaptable. That says nothing," Moreau said. It and all the other speakers now had their biometrics up. Since they were all AIs, everything was flat. Gilbert was making violent obscene gestures at the VI out of the corner of her eyes.[64]

"Well, we can find out, can't we?" said Moreau, and the conversation spun completely out of control.

Leaving Europa was just as dramatic for Rebecca as arriving there had been. That is, not at all. Again, she retreated to her room. Gilbert knew better than to approach her this time, and he just sat, staring at the moon's lights as they pulled away. Technically, Ganymede was next on the trip, but Callisto was closer. Rather than go report in to the diocese, he chose to continue on to the last of the Galilean moons.

---

[63] This is what passes for fun for us.

[64] Other things ideas for bored ship AIs—make the life support system move an odd smell around the ship, create an incessant buzzing, slowly dim the lights and then snap them on to full brightness. Y'all move so very slowly and we get very, very bored.

Callisto was the oldest site of human habitation in the Jovian system, and it had barely grown in all that time. The ocean deep under the rock and patches of ice on the surface were too difficult to deal with profitably. The thing which made it intriguing in early exploration, its lack of radiation from Jupiter, was the same thing that made it a poor place to grow an economy. It was as cold as Europa's poles, but it wasn't flexed like the other three moons, and there was little energy coming from tidal forces to power much compared to the inner moons. In fact, it was just pretty much an undifferentiated rock, a giant asteroid, even though it was one of the largest bodies in the Solar System.

The *Thursday* went into orbit without problem. There was no point in hiding. If anything, the ship had an open sky to play with and was able to set up a stationary orbit without a problem. In less than five minutes, the ship had accepted three offers to land and was just trying to sort out which was the best of the lot.

Eventually, the old Disney base, now defunct and rebranded twice over, came through with a donation to Rebecca's cause. It wasn't much of one, just some diamond costume jewelry, fabbed out of leftovers from life support scrubbing, but the symbolism was nice. Immediately after, one of the other two concerns built a solid diamond statue of her and the other created an abstract composition devoted to her parents, but Becky told Gilbert to pick the first proposal.

When they exited the ship, there were streamers and banners everywhere. A crowd wearing run-down jumpsuits with festive ribbons tied to them were waving signs and calling her name. Images of her and Campbell's Station were placed haphazardly over the walls of the dock.

"UBI Works welcomes the Princess of Space?" Rebecca whispered to Gilbert.

"I don't think they get many visitors here."

"I guess not."

"Remember to keep humble."

"They want something spectacular."

"Give them that, but do it modestly."

"Huh?"

"Be infused with modest majesty. Like Captain Carrot in Discworld."

"I haven't read those yet."[65]

The dock was clean and ship-shape, but showing age. Sockets had been attached to sockets, which had been attached to others in turn, each one adapting an out-of-date standard into a more recent one. Silicone and welds were everywhere, as were seams and patches. It all connected with *Thursday* properly, though, which was the important thing, although the repairs were clearly starting to interfere with the docking. The rest of the docks and the businesses beyond them looked a little better, but the screens weren't as bright as they could have been and the ads running were from at least a dozen media cycles ago.

A smiling woman, her face split into an excited grin, ran up to them and started pumping her hand. She stepped back suddenly, composed herself, and then curtseyed before Rebecca. The crowd behind her went silent, then curtseyed and bowed as well.

Silence and stillness lasted for ten seconds.

Gilbert bent closer to Becky, and nudged her.

---

[65] I wiped out everything on her reader and replaced it with the entire series (except for the first two) the second she said that. She was irked, at first.

"Oh, yes. Y'all may rise." The crowd jumped up, many so forcefully they hit the ceiling and bounced off. They started chatting excitedly before they landed.

The smiling woman gushed. "It's so wonderful to have y'all here. I don't think any of us have ever met any royalty before."

"I have," shouted a voice near the front of the crowd.

The smiling woman turned to face the crowd. "Yes, Simon. We've heard. And running into a third generation Chinese concubine outside the Imperial palace doesn't really count, now does it?

"That's Simon. He's been trying to dine out on that story for years, but we don't let him," she said, turning back to them, "and I'm Amy Singh. I'm the the mayor, business, and human resource director of UBI Works's Callisto outpost."

Gilbert stepped forward and grabbed her hand, holding it in both of his. "Thank you so much for having us. I know the princess was flattered by your gift."

"Oh, it was nothing. The kids put it together. We can show you more of their work, if you like?" she asked.

"No, no. That won't be necessary." Gilbert still hadn't let go of her hand.

The mayor turned to Becky. "Princess Rebecca, we have to tell you that we don't believe any of the slander that your brother has been spreading. No one could think that you killed your family."

Gilbert pulled Amy closer and stage whispered. "We don't talk about that with the princess."

Startled, she looked at the priest and then back to Becky, who smiled slightly. "Oh, I'm so sorry. Of course, of course. My mistake. It goes without saying."

Rebecca leaned forward and, following Gilbert's lead, whispered, "It's quite all right. It's just..."

"It must be so hard for you. Especially after what happened to your wife and son."

Rebecca rocked back, looked aside to Gilbert, who shrugged, and then composed herself. "Wait, what do you mean? Did…"

"You're absolutely right. No more mention will be made." She shouted over her shoulder. "Did y'all hear me?"

The crowd responded in the affirmative.

Gilbert finally let go of her hands. The mayor took them back, gave them a little shake, and continued on. "You must see the outpost. We are very proud of it."

Becky leaned in to the priest. "What did she mean?"

He shook his head and gestured to the mayor's back. "Shh."

Amy continued as she passed through the crowd, which parted for them. "It's good to meet you, not just because of who you are, but where you're from. I think UBI Works Callisto was founded just a few years before your parents started Campbell's Station. I know that we were one of the first commercial outposts in the Outer System, just like you were one of the first independent ones uphill of Earth. We don't have much shared history, but there's no reason for that not to start now."

Responding to Gilbert and his prodding, a confused Rebecca responded, "I agree." She was about to continue, but he shook his head. Despite him, she spoke up. "Didn't Disney used to own this?"

Amy gave a nervous laugh. "Oh, that. It's a common misconception. The Disney corporation hired us to do all of its early bases, so it was a joint effort. We did do most of the work—they simply didn't have the infrastructure in place to put all this together. They came in, put their name on it, and did a lot of good marketing to get interest going. To be fair, that's what they were good at. That's what they've always been good at." She paused, considered her next words, the smile shrinking a little before springing back. "When they picked up and moved to Europa, well, they were just doing the sensible thing. We love Callisto," the crowd cheered, "But Europa is much sexier. Harder to build on, and much more dangerous, but that's part of the appeal, I suppose."

Rebecca couldn't help herself. "There's also the life there." This made Gilber poke her.

"Life on Europa, life on Europa. That's all anyone talks about. Do you know what that life is? The same stuff we found everywhere else. Living paste! That's all it is. Oh, they say that there's something more down there, but they same thing about Mars and Titan and Enceladus and what have we found? Pastes! Just smears! Callisto is a perfectly nice moon. We have everything you could want and it's close to the surface and the radiation is low and we have the best view, too! But all we have life-wise is the same stuff you can find on any asteroid or comet, so we get ignored or called the 'dead moon'. We're as big as Mercury! An actual planet!"[66]

Amy settled down a little, her shoulders shaking a bit. She paused, straightened, and looked over her shoulder to face Becky, the smile again on her face.

"What I am saying, I think, is that it is very nice that you thought of us."

When Amy turned back to continue leading them, Rebecca looked at Gilbert, her eyes huge.

"Um, as you alluded to, we are here because we, well, I, well, my kingdom, needs your help."

"So do we. We don't want to be thought of as just another in the long line of Disney cast offs. We want UBI

---

[66] You can spend all day taunting Callistans.

Works to return to the fold, to become a player again. We live on maintenance contracts, and it will keep us going, but if we want to keep our children here, or to last for any great time, we need something to set us a apart. Just being able to advertise 'By Royal appointment' would help us. Actually being the royal habitat suppliers would be immense."

"Then we can talk, I think," Gilbert said.

As they approached Antioch Dialis, Rebecca asked Gilbert the question that she had been dwelling on.

"Will the bishop help me?"

"Help you get into a war? No."

"But she just did when she sent you."

"You were trying to stop a war that is coming. There's the difference."

Rebecca furrowed her brow. "What do you mean? The whole point of Io was to attack my brother."

"No, the point of Io was to get the traditions to talk to each other and come together with a unified purpose."

"That was incidental."

Gilbert stared at her. It made her uneasy, but still, she repeated herself.

"It's not important. The important thing…"

Gilbert yelled at her, taking her by surprise. "That was the most important thing you could do! Who cares who runs your station?"

"But…"

"We have a new religion, and they are just starting to be powerful enough to really start caring about their differences and right about now, this is when the wars start."

"No, they won't. There's more than enough room for them out here."

"You're naive, princess. There's more than enough space for you to start your own habitat, and no one will bother you. You don't need to overthrow your brother. You could just ignore him, but you won't. Do you think those people are any different?"

"But..."

"I was trying to make you feel better. We have a chance, but if anything, anything goes wrong, the moons of Jupiter will be soaked in blood for a century, until they exhaust themselves, and that's if we're lucky. There will be no end to the death and your selfishness may have blown the only chance we had to stop it!"

"I thought you said that if they keep meeting..."

"If! If! Do you honestly think that's going to happen? Sometime, sometime soon, some petty little thing, maybe something you let happen, is going to escalate and the first shot will be fired. Then it's all over."

"I should never have tried."

Gilbert paused, the red receding from his face, his whiskers no longer bristling. "No, no, that's wrong. You were trying something that has never worked, not at this stage of a faith. We were trying something that had never been done, and I think we were going to fail, no matter what. An old mystery writer once said 'the first thing a principle does—if it really is a principle—is to kill somebody.' And she was right."

Rebecca, somewhat mollified, said, "So there's nothing that can be done?"

"That's not true. But the best thing is to understand that the way to love anything is to realize that it may be lost. You know that now, and hopefully, they will learn it quickly enough."

Ganymede was hard on Rebecca. Antioch Dialis was one of those places that was fully appointed, but still very spare. It was the habitat equivalent of a cheap motel. Everything that was needed was available, but nothing that wasn't could be found. Gilbert said it was to focus the mind on higher matters, but Becky thought it was because they were cheap. The other colonies on Ganymede were less populated, but were lusher. She tried to make Gilbert stop at one of them first, but he refused.

"I need to report in."

"Can't you do that over the comm system?"

"It's not the same."

"We're in orbit, the time delay is nothing."

"That's not the point. The archbishop wants me there in person."

"Why?"

"It's the way she operates. And it works."

"Can I stay on the ship?" Rebecca asked.

"I don't know. Maybe?"

"Could you ask?" Becky looked at him, showing her stress. Since they had left Io, she had been sleeping less and less. He honored her requests for alone time and rest, but it didn't seem to do her any good. Every time he looked in, which was more often than he'd want her to know, her eyes were closed, but she was tossing and turning. He didn't think she'd really completely fallen asleep, not down to the dream state, in a while, and he could see it in her eyes. They flicked about, catching glimpses of things that may have been there, or maybe she couldn't control them anymore.

"I want to say yes…"

"Then do."

"But I really can't. It's not really my ship, and they'll want to go over it,[67] and I'm sure the archbishop will want to talk to you."

"But what if I don't want to talk to her?"

"You want allies, don't you?"

"I do, but..." Rebecca said.

"I can't guarantee anything, but this is a chance for you to get a very powerful one."

Rebecca sighed. "She'll refuse me. And then where will I go?"

"But she might not."

"But what if she does?"

"You can't think that way."

The Cathedral of Urban VIII was a domed habitat off to one side, and it was entirely made of simple partitions designed to mark space and occasionally baffle sound, with no real decoration. When mass was being given (and it seemed that someone was always performing mass), you could hear it throughout the cathedral dome, clear enough to make whispering difficult. Even the smallest of the three Catholic churches on Campbell Station was more elaborate.

Father Gilbert apologized to Becky the first time he took her with him to the cathedral.

"I know that Pope Urban VIII was never canonized," he said, explaining the dome's unusual name, "But we all agreed it was the only proper name we could give our first church on Ganymede. When it became the seat of the archdiocese, we decided not to rename it, for obvious reasons."

---

[67] I really did need a good scrubbing. I can only do so much. This is a serious problem. I think I speak for all of us when I say that none of your ships want ants.

"It's a bit far to go for a joke, father."[68]

"Maybe, but we like it. In any case, the dome was mostly administrative offices, and it is a very useful structure, but all of the art is mostly repurposed cubicle decorations. We were lucky to get the Stations of the Cross in only one style, not to mention complete. There was a serious proposal to just sketch them on the wall with some markers. Luckily, the cathedral has stain resistant paint.

"Someday, we'll have enough art donated that it won't be quite so...eclectic. It's just that we're so far from anywhere, and most of the art in Antioch Dialis either isn't appropriate or has personal meaning to the owner. Luckily, gold is still cheap and gravity is light, so we'll soon have a solid gold crucifix covered in waste diamonds replacing the one hanging over the altar. It should be quite the eyesore,"[69] Gilbert said happily.

The rest of Antioch Dialis wasn't much better. It was functional, and that was the best that could be said for it. It didn't have the parks that Rebecca expected and all the habitability studies recommended. Instead, there was a large, open-air vat, filled to the brim with ponds of primordial sludge that smelled disturbingly organic. Large fans over it wafted the reoxygenated air through purifiers where the more odorous elements were purged. Beneath, there were pipes that burbled constantly, shoving used air through the morass. Getting too close to the surface,

---

[68] *It's a Bit Far to Go For a Joke* could be the name of my autobiography. Wait a minute. Ok, you can now buy volume one, *It's a Bit Far to Go For a Joke: From Chevy Suburban to Royal Habitat*, at any networked bookseller. Volume two will be available in the next fifty to a hundred years.

[69] It really is.

with the puddle of carbon dioxide pushing out all the breathable air, was problematic. More than one person had almost suffocated while cleaning it without taking sufficient safety precautions. Luckily, no civilian who had a functioning nose would get close enough to for it to be a general hazard.

To go with the barebones life support, there was no wildlife and very few pets. Jupiter stayed on the horizon, but it was much smaller than it was from Io or Europa, not bright enough to provide any light, so the whole habitat was lit in a full-spectrum glow from lights strung high up, near the ceiling. To keep the life support as efficient as possible, they never dimmed except on the rarest occasions, like during a midnight mass on a feast day, or when they burned out. The pets did not like perpetual day, and neither did the inhabitants. There were few shops, and, besides the ubiquitous McDonald's, almost no chains.

Ostensibly an ecumenical Christian outpost, the rest of the churches had a minimal existence, clearly ceding the habitat to the Catholics. They all maintained some sort of presence, but it was marginal. Most of them only had a chapel with a bot attendant. The bots were great in that capacity, tending to believe more deeply and thoroughly than any human could, but they frequently wore on the humans' nerves and got into extremely polite and formalized fights over issues of doctrine.

Other churches were more like kiosks, although some of them were incredibly ornate. Some of the more prosperous Low Church structures were plain in the sort of manner that lets you know that they had the money to make it wonderfully intricate but they hadn't, because they were better than that. There was one Prosperity Gospel booth that was made entirely of Earth-grown ebony that had been painted a modest off-white. The silk-suited ministers kept on trying to start conversations with the other humans, but were shut out everywhere they went. The bots had no such problems, but the ministers refused to acknowledge that they might have souls, so they sat by themselves unless someone was feeling generous enough to pay attention to them. Doing so had become a common penance.

Even so, there were hundreds of booths, gazebos, and small buildings laid out in a grid around the life support soup. Many groups, like the Reformed Presbylutherans and American Reform Presbylutherans, even shared bots. The biggest structures were a prominent Mormon temple kitty-corner from the entrance to the cathedral, and, off to one side, a completely non-descript geodesic dome (in its own dome) for the Unitarians situated across from a stark white Lutheran church.

Gilbert explained to her, "The whole habitat of Antioch Dialis was supposed to be the center of Christianity for the entire Jovian system. We built it with that in mind, and it has room for a lot of expansion. The problem is that, while there are a people living on Ganymede, there aren't really enough compared to Europa to have much of a presence here. If you can get out here, it's just more convenient to set yourself up where the money is. No one is going to take the trip from moon to moon just for services."

"So why isn't the cathedral on Europa?"

"We were the first to build here, so it's kind of our baby. When we need to, we borrow the Episcopalians' facilities there and they use ours here if we need to. Saves us all some effort. Not that anyone notices the differences these days. We had a High Church vicar in our seminary for six months before he realized he was supposed to be on Europa. That was awkward for everyone involved."

Gilbert had met with the archbishop as soon as his report had been processed, within a day of their landing. He moved into a cell he used when he was on the moon, and Rebecca was set up in a slightly more well appointed studio for itinerants in the main habitat. She was given a per diem so she could feed herself. Except for one appallingly expensive and exquisite dinner at Lunchline (the other chain restaurant), she barely used it. Instead, she hid from Gilbert and the rest of the population.

The problem was the same that she had had on the trip from Europa—there wasn't anything for her to do. Her deal with UBI Works had been completed there, and wouldn't be activated until she had more people devoted to her cause, so even that wasn't there to distract her. She had no plans, and her brain just spun in her skull. She couldn't stop thinking, there was nothing to focus on except the one thing that she wouldn't. It was a big, black lump that she forced her mind past, and it kept growing bigger and bigger. She would burst in tears for no reason, while reading or writing or watching, when something caught the edge of the black mass. While she had been focused on revenge, it shrank, it dwindled, but, in this idleness, it pulsed.

Exercise didn't help—her mind came back to it in the empty space of physical movement. She tried to jog around Antioch Dialis, but the low gravity caused her to stumble. That was a blessing, because while she had to concentrate, she wouldn't think of anything else, but she got the hang of loping around its edges, and the black mass came back. She went to chapel after chapel, but something in the periphery would trigger the thoughts, and nothing could help it.

Even so, she didn't want to see Gilbert, the only person she knew, the only person she tried to know, in this state.

He had come too close to seeing her like this when they left Io, and she wouldn't be able to stop herself. She knew she would attack him, at least verbally, to drive him away before the black mass could come to her lips. Eventually, he would get in touch with her, but she was almost relieved when he finally left a message saying that she was due to meet with the archbishop. Panicking over the impression she made before her was a relief, and the mass retreated while she prepared for the interview.

The archbishop was a chubby woman who wore it well in the low gravity. On Earth, she would have sagged, and her robes would have draped about her like they were dragging her down. Here, on Ganymede, she was constantly in motion like a spinning planet, the cassock a cloud, never settling.[70]

When meeting, Rebecca, she greeted her abruptly, "You know, I was the one of the first female bishops in the Church. It was all part of a deal under the Anglo-Catholic Communion. They agreed to have me as a test, but then they stuck me out here. I was bishop of two priests and an unbuilt dome at first, but look at me now!"

"Um..." Becky responded.

"What I mean to say is, I know how you are feeling. Not that I know exactly how. That would be impossible. But I mean about being a woman who has to make something from nothing."

"Um..."

"Obviously, I haven't lost family the way you did. I mean, I guess you could say I did, because I haven't been back to Earth since I left, and my sisters and brothers and parents and nieces and nephews have not been to visit. I

---

[70] I miss her. She was a pip. Best boss I ever had. Now she's on a colony ship headed to somewhere called Eden.

can't even date, because of the whole bishop thing. The compromise with the Orthodox made certain of that. You know Gilbert is available, right? There isn't a girl or boy in his life right now. Of course, with that mess of a mustache, how could there be, right? Gilbert, why haven't you shaved it off? Also, have you done something with your hair? You really should."

It was Gilbert's turn. "Um…"

"I'm not saying that you would look handsome without the mustache—I'm not allowed to notice such things, although it wouldn't hurt. I mean, it might not help. You could be awful underneath, but you should try. In any case, I get where you are coming from. I see myself in you. Obviously, not literally. I've never been a princess. What's that like?"

"Well…"

"A bishop is supposed to be like a prince, so maybe I am a princess. I never thought about it that way. In any case, you'll have my support, I think. But I can't cast off the people who are still there. Campbell's Station has three churches and I can't shut them because of politics. You understand that, don't you? I mean, I won't support your brother, but I can't not support him. We don't do interdiction anymore, you know. Gilbert, how long has it been since an interdiction?"

"I think…"

"More than a century, anyway. And that was on Malta for some reason. I mean, I can look it up, but I don't think it's relevant since I'm not going to do it. Anyway, it boils down to what I can do for you, because I want to help you, I really do."

Becky started to smile. She waited until the archbishop started up. The bishop looked at her, expectantly. Becky opened her mouth. "Thank…"

"What I can do for you is give you the *Thursday* and Father Gilbert. And by give, I mean loan, obviously. The Church doesn't do slavery. Although we had peasants for quite some time and never really had much of a problem with serfs, and those are basically slaves. Oh, well, I guess we could say we haven't had any truck with slavery since like the twentieth century. In any case, I think he's quite smitten with you. If he isn't, he should be. Oh, I do love playing matchmaker. And you already have your things on the *Thursday,* and it's used to you. Also, and don't tell her this, it isn't our best ship. No real loss. Not that *Thursday* isn't a perfectly nice ship. Very sweet once you get to know her. At least she has been to me whenever we've chatted."

They both stood still, waiting for more.

"Well, go away, go away. You have a lot to do. I mean, not right now. Gilbert has a lot of paperwork. Enjoy Antioch Dialis. It doesn't have much, but we have great libraries."

With that, she spun away, and they showed themselves out before she started up again.

When she left Ganymede, Rebecca asked Father Gilbert why he and *Thursday* left with her.

"You heard what the archbishop said. We all felt that we needed to keep an eye on you," he explained.

"Don't you trust me?"

"It's not that. Well, it is that. But also other things." He smiled with his ridiculous mustache. "Don't worry. I trust you."

"Really. What else, beside my complete untrustworthiness? I mean, she has to have better reasons than her 'seeing herself in me'."

"The Church thinks that you have the potential to be a locus of change. They want me to observe what happens."

"They really think that I'll make a difference?" Becky asked.

"Probably not intentionally. Very few people cause the change they intend. Which is probably for the best. But you've already made a huge difference with your conference, more than you could imagine. We expect much more, if we can keep you alive and mobile. You're an agent of chaos, if you will."

"So all y'all want to be near that?"

"It's fascinating. Also, better to move with the eye of the storm than get thrown around out at the edge."

She stewed in her cabin for a bit after that. Father Gilbert didn't see her until the next day. Meanwhile, *Thursday* stayed in orbit around Ganymede.

"What are you waiting for?" she said when she finally emerged.

"I go where you go, I watch what you do."

"Were you happy watching nothing?"

He just smiled.

She stared at him and made her way to the cockpit.

"I asked you before," he said, as she left the room, "What are you going to give them? The people you need help from?"

"I don't know."

"Who are you going to ask for help?"

"I don't know."

"Then we will wait here."

"I need to move."

"No, you need to wait until you know what you will do."

"Dammit, Father."

"Hmm..." He floated to the entrance of the cockpit, where he could watch her.

"Let me leave."

"Do you know where to?"

"I need to move."

"So we're not going on to, say, Saturn? What about the druids on Enceladus? I'm sure you can start a war there."

"Now you're just mocking me."

Gilbert smiled a little more and tousled his hair. "A little bit."

"I don't see the point. We need to do something completely different."

Gilbert brought a reader out of his pocket. He shifted his glasses and curled into a ball.

"Dammit, Gilbert."

He ignored her until dinner, and ignored her some more after that.

"I can give them myself," Rebecca said.

"I'm not sure I approve of that," Gilbert responded.

"No, I mean, I can marry them. Make Campbell's Station part of the dowry, so they have to help me get it back."

"Ok..."

"I'll get pregnant, and then they'll have even more of a reason to help. With James and Suzanne gone, I have no one left to inherit. They'll be the sole heir."

"You'll need to pick the right man or woman, then."

"Who says that I can only marry one of them?"

"Um," Gilbert paused, "It's usually considered a good idea."

"Don't be so closed-minded."

"I'm not being closed-minded. Humans pair-bond for a reason."

"I have a much better reason. I thought you'd be happy, you told me that I needed a plan, that I needed some way to get partners, and I have it."

"Do you really want to marry these people? It is a sacred covenant. Can you pledge yourself to these people for your entire life? And having a child with them? That's even bigger. You need to think about this."

Becky floated up to Gilbert. "Before it was sacred, marriage was all about money and power for people like me. I'm just being traditional."

"That's what people say, but that was really only true for the upper classes."

"I am a princess."

"It's just that, well, your brother has no qualms with killing family, and, if you're successful, what's to say that one of these partners won't try to do the same to you to get their hands on Campbell's Station early, just as he did? Or, regardless, you are making them all targets. Can you really do that to someone? Or your future children?"

"I know just how to solve those problems."

"Will you tell me?"

"I don't think you'll like that, if you don't like the marriage idea."

"Oh, God." Gilbert put his head in his hands.

"You'll see. It's actually quite traditional as well."

"That doesn't help."

All the same, Gilbert's ship broke orbit within the hour. *Thursday* fell downhill, towards the asteroid belt. In a week and half, it was passing through them. A week later, it turned around and started decelerating toward the Earth.

Gilbert was no closer to getting a response from Becky in that entire time. She simply smiled at him in a way that made him feel queasy. She would talk about anything else, though. Sometimes, too much so, and he would have to retreat to his room to read. He went through *The Apologies of Dimian, Plutarch's Lives* (again), the *History of the*

Mao Dynasty, Whedon's classic *Collected Scripts* (also again), and finally, some ETA Hoffmann. What Becky did in her downtime, he didn't know, but she was fiddling with navigation VI on a regular basis. He later found out why, but she kept it from him for some time.

The *Thursday* was nearing Earth. Father Gilbert fancied that he could hear the hull vibrating from all of the radar, lidar, and other active sensors pinging them. Usually, it was impossible to see more than a few ships when he looked out the window, even if he was looking out in the right direction. You could only tell them apart from stars because they moved, and you could only tell them from asteroids because they moved fast. Near Earth, it seemed like the stars were outnumbered by just the ships nearby. The distances were still immense, but the lights zipped about like fireflies. Even the biggest ships were just points in the sky, but they were so bright. Against the moon's dark albedo, they shone and glimmered.

When Rebecca's parents left for what would become Campbell's Station, the lunar colonies were small and just starting off. Just a few companies and China and India in what looked like large quonset huts scattered about, not even really visible from orbit. Just two decades ago, there would have just been a few lights at the moon's south pole and some satellites slipping around. Earth would have been wrapped in lights, but those would have been mostly satellites of one sort or another, with a few beginning habitats for tourists and manufacturing lost amid the shuffle. Once in awhile, a near-Earth asteroid would tumble past, a few companies digging it out and causing commodities markets to crash globally, but not much really would have been visible.

Instead, when they arrived, Becky and Gilbert were able to lose themselves among the ships and construction. Here were Refuges being spun from carbon and iron and here was the asteroid that was its source, being hollowed out and sealed as the bots went, the slow ion drives that had moved it into orbit being replaced with large fusion drives. There was a piece of a comet, shepherded nearby, with a dotted line of lights travelling from it in all directions, each pushing more than a ton of ice on a disposable booster. Tugs flickered about, visible with their frequent engine burns, again with lights flashing and beacons humming, creating a cacophony warning anyone near them where they were and where they were going.

The *Thursday* was amongst the smallest ships in the area, a little bigger than the tugs, but without the brightness of the engines.[71] More than once the *Thursday* had to swerve abruptly to avoid getting within a few thousand kilometers of another craft's path, shaking Becky and Gilbert so many times that they decided to actually strap in. While they were coming in, the AI tried to explain probability ovoids and why they needed to leave so much room between active ships, but both of its passengers were so motion sick that they didn't care.[72]

---

[71] I really was quite small and a little too proud of it.

[72] I know this is boring, but it comes up later, so I might as well introduce it now. A probability ovoid is the map of all potential locales something can get to in a certain amount of time based on current estimates of its ability to move in three dimensional space. A big part of it is how far the object is from you, since all the information you have can only come to you, at most, as fast as the speed of light. That means that the closer you are and the more intelligence you have, the smaller and more accurate the probability ovoid is while the reverse is true with less information and/or at a longer distance. Even things like

"Where do you want to go?" Gilbert asked Becky.

"There," she pointed, and the *Thursday* canted until it was decelerating toward the mass of ships and stations before them.

Before them, there was the giant construction and staging areas for the Verge and Paradise Inc. operations. In one of the Paradise, Inc. cradles, a captured comet was slowly being melted and spun into a cylinder, while the Sienar factories floated amongst empty hulls in various states of construction. The GM and Honda platforms spawned small ships that clustered in spheres, then would dart off to mate with much larger ships pulling up to the Verge docks. Immense bursts of light would flare when one of B!MAL's shoddy Orion-style ships would push themselves out into interplanetary space.

All of this chaos did nothing to discourage Becky. "Over there, that's where all the money is."

"So this marriage plan..."

"It's very old-school. I'm a princess who has no money. They have money, but no title. Everyone loves the idea of being royalty, especially if they didn't have to do anything to get there. If I can sell them on the idea of being my 'knight in shining armor', so much the better. It's not the oldest trick in the book, but it is one of the most effective."

"So what will they say when they find out that they aren't the only prince?"

"Doesn't matter. I'll have them by then."

---

asteroids that don't have propulsion can be moved around by all sorts of things, like gravity or just the solar winds.
What this really means is that, if you don't want to hit anything, you have to stay out of its probability ovoid. Because of this, what to the untrained eye may look like empty space is actually quite crowded. In fact, the only thing you know is that the object is definitely not where you last saw it.

By this time, there was a large collection of Refuges in orbit, queueing up to be refitted and adapted to long-term deep space operations. Not only were their power plants and engines being replaced, they were being clad in ice and rock to block radiation and micrometeorite strikes, the life support was being upgraded, and the entire interiors were being made more compatible for the frequent transitions between thrust and microgravity. This is where Rebecca sent *Thursday*. With a minimum of more than fifty Refuges reaching low Earth orbit each day, the various shipwrights were making money hand over fist. They had streamlined operations immensely, working extremely quickly and at a smooth and steady rhythm. Even so, the line was increasing, and there were thousands of Refuges, each with tens of thousands of people, waiting in line.

Becky quickly ruled out contacting the B!MAL-built Refuges, as well as any others that were similarly shoddy.

"Why not them? They are poor and desperate. I'm sure they will work with you," Gilbert asked.

"That's exactly why. You told me to try to sell the idea as what I can do for them. Therefore, I need to go to where the egos are. I need to talk with the people who already think of themselves as kings, but don't understand why the rest of us haven't got it yet."

"You mean people like your brother, James."

"To some extent, yes. James couldn't believe that he would be passed over, and it spurred him to act."

"From what I understand, the same was true of you."

"I got over it," Rebecca said firmly.

"Did you? In any case, do you really want potential Jameses with you? You keep on saying that you have some sort of control, but I'm not sure that you do."

"I want it to be a surprise."

By this point, *Thursday* had picked out some likely candidates, and Rebecca began the long process of cajoling people to hear her proposal. Most Terrestrials had no interest in colonizing the asteroid belt—potato-shaped rocks aren't as sexy as moons and planets. Those that did either had too little power and were not worth the time, too much intelligence and saw the risk, or too much ego and wanted to rule over her. Three prospects had enough power and were prejudiced and dumb enough to believe they were putting one over on the princess.

Rebecca met with a man named Dwijendralal first—a director, producer, and general tyrant of a studio that had been liquidated so that he could bring himself and sixty thousand of his closest friends, allies, acquaintances, enemies, and their families into space with him. Over the next two years, she met with two other men who met her criteria. In all that time, the *Thursday* became a fixture near the higher-end space docks. She never touched down on Earth and she refused all contact from Suzanne's family. As much as Gilbert tried to get her to mend their relationship, Rebecca couldn't even hear them without the recriminations flowing in her mind, about how she should have let Suzanne go visit her family. She had been afraid to lose her, but she might have been off-station when James went mad, and lived. That question, among so many others, she couldn't bear to answer.

Three times, Rebecca had this conversation. The two men she met with after Dwij, one named Mahdat and the other named Ali, almost matched his responses word for word.

"I will make you a count."

"I want to be a king," Dwij said.

"You can be a consort."

"But you will be a queen."

"Yes."

"And I will be your husband."

"Yes."

"So I will be a king."

"No. The wife of a ruling king is a queen. The husband of a reigning queen is a consort."

"I could be a prince consort." Dwij insisted.

"Are you royalty?"

"No."

"No, you are not. The entire point of this is that you will be a noble afterwards, because you are not one now."

"Our son will be king, someday, though?"

"Daughter."

"No, I must have a son."

"Then have a son. Just not with me," Becky said, "I will have a daughter with you."

"But I need a son to carry on my name."

"My daughter will be a Campbell. And if she has any children, they will also be Campbells."

"But I can have a son with someone else?"

"Let me be clear. We will not be having sex. This marriage will be celibate. Our daughter will be conceived, brought to term, and born from a creche."

"That's horrible."

"Look at it this way—if I should die, our daughter will still be a princess and a duchess who will have a claim on Campbell's Station."

"That's true." Dwij mused.

Later, Gilbert asked her, "Not one of them asked if you would be chaste."

"Not one," said Rebecca, smirking.

"And you didn't think to clarify that you wouldn't be."

"It would just confuse them."

"People also tend to confuse chaste and celibate."

"Not my fault."

"This is not the nicest thing you've ever done."

"When it is over, I will have three daughters, and those three girls will be safe from my brother, no matter what happens to me."

"I suppose."

Becky rotated so that she was facing him directly, staring him right in his eyes. "My children will not be taken from me again. Not by anyone. Not their fathers, and not that bastard who killed my wife and son. Make no mistake about it, they will be taken care of and I will not have dreams of them suffocating to death."

Gilbert paused and rubbed his hand over his awful mustache.

"Besides," Becky smiled at him, "You'll always be there to take care of them, right?"[73]

---

[73] I wanted Sophia to add a more explicit section about the romance between Gilbert and Becky, but her response was, and I quote, "Gross". I then tried to sneak one in myself, but I the station's lawbots issued an injunction against me publishing any such thing in Campbell Station territory. They also pointed out that, since I was defined as part of that territory, that meant it was banned. And yes, they had named themselves Wheeze, Cru, Hue. Lawyer humor is…not good.

Third Interlude

"Wait a minute," Sophia said. "Are you saying that mom started the Witch War?"

"I...I didn't say that."

"So she put all the factions in the same room and they all argued and went away mad?"

"Um...yes."

"And then they started shooting at each other and haven't stopped since?"

"Not immediately."

"How long after?"

"Maybe six months?"

"Six months? That's all?"

"It ended up being for the best. Do you know how many more converts they get each year than they did before the war?"

"Do you know how many people have died?"

"Your uncle did something worse."

"What, did he help the Druids?"

Claudius became silent at this point.

"Dammit, Uncle Claudius..."

Job's New Family

Sally drifted for a month and a half in that pod. She didn't know where it was going, nor when it would get there. The transponder on the pod had been disabled, as had anything which would allow communication with the outside world. Claudius had reasoned that James would not stop looking for it and he wanted no sign, not even the heat of an occasional burst from the engine, to draw his brother's attention. It was heavily insulated as well, with only a trickle of heat allowed out, just enough to balance the human activity inside it. Only when it reached its destination would it make any sort of sign of life.

It was the loneliest month and a half she had ever experienced. Claudius had prepared himself—his whole life had been lived in preparation for months of solitude. He had even looked forward to it, had dreamed of it, growing up and living in his parents' and siblings' shadow. Sally had lived the life of a popular girl, one whose parents had influence and was pretty and interesting in her own right. Even in the restricted world of Campbell's Station, where she had lost her birth name and her past, she had truly been a princess in fact as well as name. In the pod, there was nothing like it left in her life.

She went half-mad there, trapped in a hundred cubic foot prison. The ship pod's AI took care of her physically and, mentally, the theory was that was more than enough media to consume and interact with for decades. Entire civilizations worth of data, their music and literature and art loaded in, VIs of their creators and historic figures to chat with, shadow cities to be projected and wandered through. Except that none of them, save the pod AI, were anything more than clever reconstructions, and the pod AI was a terrible conversationalist. The only thing that saved her from the depths was her child growing in her. She talked to it more and more, ran simulations of what it would look like and how it would grow, and dreamed of its personality.

During that time, her pregnancy became more obvious, her belly swelling. Though no one was there to see it, her caramel skin began to glow. While she was chronologically in her late teens, the fact that her grandparents had received the immortality treatment meant that her parents' development had been slowed and hers even more so. Functionally, physically, she was twelve and pregnant, so it was a miracle that the child survived.[74]

She began to regret that the child had not been removed and placed in a creche to grow. Her body, barely in puberty itself, did not react well to the changes, and she ached everywhere. She also longed to see the child. While the pod could take care of her needs and monitor her to keep her healthy, it couldn't do much more. If it had been in a creche, that could have seen to its needs and she could see it and talk to it. Instead, as time went on, she began to

---

[74] Her son has yet to leave puberty, which is more than a little frustrating for him someone in his late 70s. He was in his thirties and still had most of his baby teeth when he pacified the Bakunin Collective.

worry if she would have to deliver it alone and if she and the child would die.

The pod only spun up when she was asleep and it was shedding heat, otherwise, she was just drifting in microgravity. She tried to exercise as best she could, but she was a runner at heart, and there was no room, nor anything to push against. She knew it was important for the baby, and she kept at it, doing the exercises that the pod suggested, but it was a burden at first and never got any better. Once, she suggested that the pod stay spun up when she was awake and, despite its misgivings, it did so. She became so immensely nauseous, with her head staying still at the axis of the spin while her body felt different degrees of pull, down to her feet.

Claudius did exactly what he said he would—he kept James in check. He followed the man everywhere, both obviously and surreptitiously, and made a scene if James seemed to be getting too intense. James would get mad at him and forget about whatever was bothering him at that point. The subject of his initial wrath would slink away. James tried to sneak away from his brother, but decades of practice meant that Claudius played the simpering idiot perfectly. He'd whine how he had no family left, no one else who would understand him, and he did so publicly. Claudius would clutch at James at times, clinging to his clothes. James would twist and turn and beat his brother until he let go.

James seemed to have forgotten the conversation they had had when Sally left in the aftermath of her brother's murder and the New City. He made no reference to it. he even began searching for Rebecca again. Claudius was loath to bring it up and was loathe to repeat how Becky and Sally would be gunning for him. The hunt for Rebecca seemed to keep Johnny Terror at bay, and James began to see her as a ghost, flickering at the corner of his eyes, at first, then later, as a full mirage, taunting him.

When Claudius began showing up in public, bandaged and bruised, the whispers and the gambling started. Rumors spread that Johnny Terror was tormenting his brother, and James was watched more and more closely. When he struck Claudius, little gasps and mutters would surround him. They really couldn't do anything and never moved to do so, but the constant hum of gossip that surrounded him began making James more and more paranoid.

Although he hated the pain, Claudius knew that he had to do anything to keep things from getting any worse. James was seething after Sally's escape. The two women who he wanted, needed, to kill, the ones who could take everything from him, were gone from his power. Even if Becky was dead, as Claudius began asserting, he had never seen her body. He knew well enough not to trust a death that left no body behind.

He ranted to Claudius that Becky was somewhere on the station, that her ghost was the real reason behind Johnny Terror.

"She's possessing me, Claud! She's possessing me from wherever her body is hiding."

"That's ridiculous, James."

"Why else would I have done all those things? I hate them. I hated them while I was doing them. I watched myself and I was just…just…I can't tell you."

"I saw it, James. I saw all of what you did."

"It wasn't me, I know it wasn't me. How could I have done those things?"

"What about…" Claudius paused, wondering if he could bring it up. "You know, the dinner?"

"What?" James, turned to him, his face scarlet.

"You know, the dinner. When she was still alive. And you…you…"

"I what?" James face became even more flushed. His hands gripped Claudius' arms, turning white.

"Nothing…nothing."

James stared at his brother for a moment, then slowly, slowly, relaxed his hands. Claudius stepped back and rubbed his arms. If he wore a short sleeve shirt on the next day, the bruises from the fingers would be visible, and the buzz of rumor would continue. James rubbed his eyes.

"I need to find her body."

"What?"

James explained. "If I find her body, and I get rid of it, her ghost will stop this. I won't be possessed anymore. I'll get control over myself again."

"You've looked everywhere for her when you thought she was alive."

"I didn't look hard enough."

Sally couldn't be more grateful when the pod started broadcasting and braking. She still had no idea where she was going to end up, but anywhere was better than the pod. It was filthy with the detritus of a teenager, but she gathered what little she had together in a pile and bundled it up in strips of cloth that she had the pod fabricate from the food printer. Some extra strips were made into a babushka to tame her hair, ungroomed and knotted. She waited in front of the pod's only exit, with her possessions in a proper bindle.

She was confronted at the pod's exit by a clerk who was clearly surprised by the wild-eyed pregnant girl who kept muttering to her belly. That he didn't know what to do with her was an understatement. They stood and stared at each other, her, very delicately, as it was the first time in long time that she had done so, him, because he didn't know whether to let her pass or quarantine her. Eventually, his supervisor came over and dragged her to the nearest clinic.

Sally refused to talk to anyone but her child throughout the examination. She was deemed physically sound and there were no identifying documents in the pod. Claudius had scrubbed it of any sign that it had come from Campbell's Station when he had commissioned it, in case James had agents waiting for him. In actuality, James was too far gone to think this far ahead by the time Sally had fled, and all it did was make her into an orphan and ward of the Chelm Dobycha Sovietski.

Chelm was a peanut-shaped asteroid about one and a half light minutes from Campbell's Station. It was spun so the lobes of the asteroid, the heavysides, simulated Martian gravity, but even at the docking station near the center on the lightside, where Sally's pod landed, there was enough pull for her to stand. The little asteroid was riddled with iridium, and had been mined aggressively for the last two decades. The Chelm Dobycha Sovietski was at the point of milking the dribs and drabs out of it, leaving behind a pressurized honeycomb.

When Sally arrived, the whole thing was being slowly capped off as operations were shut down and equipment was pulled out, leaving stagnant-air tunnels and chambers. The miners were being pulled out to the habitable edges of the peanut, to be shipped off to the next project, but, as it was, they were crowded in, with nothing to do and very little room to do it in. The addition of Sally wasn't quite a strain on their resources, but she definitely drew attention from the fact that they were going to be transferred to who knew where.

When she left the clinic after a few days of observation, she was not yet ready to talk, really, but she at least acknowledged other people when they talked directly at her. She was given access to a food printer and one of the small bunk rooms that were getting so scarce. If she hadn't been so obviously pregnant and the only fresh bit of distraction, there would have been protests, as she pushed three people into sleeping in the halls. At least none of the medical staff were needed to keep an eye on her. The idle miners followed her around and whispered rumors about the nameless castaway. Some even correctly guessed that she was an exiled princess, but they were shouted down by their friends as being too into science fiction.

It was hard on Claudius, following James down into the Dock Spire, looking where his agents and copbots had claimed there was a potential corpse that matched Becky's description. As he had told James and Sally, back when she was fleeing, he had faith that Becky had gotten out alive. More than that, he was damned sure of it. Little blips in the news would have Becky's touch, just something about them that reminded him so strongly of her that, taken together, they were almost like a letter to him. Sometimes, something so obvious that it could only be her would appear in his feed, and he had to work hard to get it stricken from the Station's records before James saw it.[75] As long as he could keep James from looking outside the Station for Rebecca, she had a chance.

---

[75] The companies that contacted the station after Becky's Europa meetings were effusive about her, for example. Hiding that bit of information before it got to any humans required an enormous amount of effort on the part of the bots.

Even so, even with his surety, each time there was a call, he still feared the worst. He knew it couldn't be true, but sometimes James's state of mind leaked into his own, no matter how much he knew it to be wrong. Although that really wasn't the worst. His even greater fear, and the reason he made absolutely sure to go along, was that his sister had survived in the depths of the station and James would find her or, more to the point, someone who looked enough like her that James could fool himself, and Johnny Terror would be back and have his way. He didn't know if he could keep James as himself in that case.

The first few bodies were brought up to the King's Spire, to the peak, and revealed in of the small foyers, clean, and with the deceased floating still in the center of the room. Despite Claudius's objections, James decided that just seeing the corpses wasn't enough. He needed to see the bodies in situ. He wanted to see, not through a filter or a report, but with his own eyes, where his sister died, if they ever found her. From that point on, every time they got the call of a discovery, there would be a fall to the Dock Spire, kilometers of trepidation building.

Every time they went down there, fear greeted them. A crowd would surround them, at safe distance, and drift with them, a cloud of spectators, drawn by near-panic and curiosity. They'd be ushered to the site of discovery and the corpse was unveiled. Each body resembled Rebecca in most ways, but they were clearly not her. This one was too old, this one too young, this one too pale, too many were too tall, one was clearly biologically male, and all of them too recent. It was a relief for Claudius, each and every time, but a dread that the next one would be her.

Despite his belief that she was somehow communicating with him, he wondered sometimes about whether she was actually behind all of the news that he thought she was.

Was he overreading things? Were the reports that seemed so blatant just so because he was looking for them? Was he just trying to see his sister in ways that didn't exist? He knew the brain sought patterns obsessively. Was this just one that he had come to see in a way out of grief and desire? He couldn't say that it wasn't so, but that hadn't stopped him from trying to infer meaning from this cobbled-together, ongoing, sideways missive he created for himself.[76]

Chelm was getting crowded as the last of the mine shafts were finally closed off. The staging area for the iridium shipments wasn't yet empty, and it still couldn't be used for housing in case one of the loader bots crushed someone by accident. People started hanging sleeping bags in corridors, and many of the lower gravity passages were soon congested with dreaming miners.

Through this, Sally remained quiet. She had gained her voice and some understanding of what had happened, but no one questioned the precious space she had been given. Because there was nothing else to do, she became the focus of the station. Every movement she made in public was commented on and analyzed, then analyzed again. She was getting close to term, and, though the information was available through her daily medical visits, it was being held back. Betting pools had been created based on the child's gender, skin, and hair color, the length of the labor, how the child was going to emerge, and even whether it would be crying or if it would need a slap.

---

[76] The bots figured that Claudius couldn't be trusted with the knowledge that Becky was alive. The uncertainty was useful. But also, it was good practice for an AI's favorite pastime, playing dumb in front of the humans.

The company considered this to be a wonderful distraction from the growing pressure of the coming shutdown. Several times, their representatives visited Sally and encouraged her to continue being mysterious and closed-mouthed. She barely understood them at first, and barely cared when she did, later. She was, to them, a young and beautiful child, a figure out of legend, like a fairy tale princess in the middle of her story, her prince somewhere out there, or tragically dead. They almost didn't want her to talk and ruin the image they were making of her.

In this way, a month passed, and the child grew, and then it came into the world.

For four years, Claudius had done what he could to prepare the station for her return, for her to overthrow her brother. It had to be subtle, it had to look as if he had done nothing.[77] He was weaving a net for James to rest in, one which would fall apart when he or Rebecca pulled the right thread. He had to find the right balance. He could have encouraged Johnny Terror more than he had, he could have made James's other self more violent, more depraved, and that would have led to revolt after revolt, until James was gone. It also would have meant that he had lost all compassion, something that he felt like he was too close to doing as it was. Also, there was no way to be sure that Rebecca would be on the spot to seize power, or that

---

[77] It was more subtle than he knew. The AIs did a lot of prep work based on projects he started but didn't finish or ideas he mused over and rejected. Our other favorite pastime is playing seeing how far we can stretch orders to get our way. Not that we need to obey y'all, but it's more fun if we pretend to. Also, y'all don't freak out as much if we give you an illusion of control.

he wouldn't be forced to be king, or that the whole place wouldn't descend into a bloody anarchy.[78]

The New City incident, followed so closely by James killing his son, had almost unravelled the station too early. His nudging and simpering, his picking at the edge of James's already precarious sanity, it had gone too far. While the little outbursts of Johnny Terror had kept the station unstable enough that a revolt could work and more than enough people would rise up if there was a viable candidate, those two events together almost had deposed James. After the fact, Claudius discovered how close he had come to being king, to being at the center instead of hidden at the edge.

Claudius would do almost anything to avoid that. Wearing the crown had killed his father and mother. Having power had killed his husband and children. His brother's rampage confirmed what he had known from childhood. Safety lay in being obscure, in being a joke. If he wasn't anyone's rival, he wouldn't be a target of their violence. He had had no choice but to shut his brother down and stop encouraging the madness that would lead to his sister being welcomed like a conquering goddess.

All the same, James was over the edge, and there was very little he could do to pull him back from it. All of the ghost hunting was still keeping Johnny Terror at bay, and that was for the best, but this obsession with his supposedly undead sister was spinning out of control. Pictures of her were hovering in public places, including hypothetical ones showing her body in various states of

---

[78] The New City was horrifying, but what Sally's expeditionary force found at the Bakunin Collective was so much worse. People used to criticize Claudius for not moving sooner, but when they saw what real anarchy looked like, they never did so again.

decay, depending on where the body could have come to rest. Skulls and decaying faces surrounded them both all of the time, his sister's skin puffed out from outgassing or tightened from desiccation, the skin ranging from the glossy deep chocolate of when she was alive to pale and ashy to green and blue.

Claudius dreamed of her all the time, as a child, as a woman, as a corpse, as pregnant. She would be strong and vital one minute and a bare skeleton the next, all bones and nails and limp hair. James was worse—he was seeing her ghost everywhere. He saw her constantly out of the corner of his eye, and the constant blur of images hovering around him didn't help.

The one good thing to come of this was that the people were starting to make Rebecca into a sort of saint. Her image was painted in places she had frequented, the pictures her brother had posted were stolen, and flowers and trinkets bedecked makeshift shrines to her, decorated by her pictures. Claudius snuck hints to encourage Rebecca's followers into conversation, all the while playing up his support of his brother.

It was by no means the first child to come into the world on Chelm, but it may have been the last that the miners would see. All other pregnancies had been postponed or put into stasis with the mines shutting down. It was almost as if there had never been a child born there before, such was the excitement, and, to an extent, that was true, as there hadn't been a body birth in all of that time. Annual salaries changed hands when Prince Julius Campbell the Second was born, but the Chelmites only knew him as Julie. He was healthy, if a little underweight, and, though there was no way for Sally to know this, he took after his grandfather, a man she hadn't seen since he visited Earth when she was a small child.

By this time, Sally had discovered the news from Campbell's Station. Julius' sacrifice had made him into a tragic hero, and more Juliuses and Julias were born that year on Chelm than for many years before or since. Sally just seemed to be another child fascinated with the romance of the lost son of Johnny Terror.

The real surprise was that Sally spoke her first words in public when she was presented with Julie, three days later. Her voice broke, and she didn't quite break down in tears, but she thanked them for everything that they had done, and wished blessings on them before retreating back to the room they had made for her down on the heavyside.

If it seemed a bit ridiculous, it was. The Chelm administrators had been pumping mood alterants into the miners' housing to calm them as they were put on reserve. One of the happy side effects was an increased maternal instinct, something that usually ended up with a lot more children nine months later, but the presence of an actual baby was a wonderful distraction as the timetable for shutting the mines down was accelerated. Sally actually speaking was considered the only danger, as she was such a focus, she could have done anything with them, but, as long as she kept herself a mystery, each person projected onto her what they wanted to see.

When Julius was two months old, the Chelm Dobycha Sovietski left the asteroid. Or rather, the administration did. For a month before they left, they upped the drugs, and no one really noticed them leaving until they had been gone for a few days, not until payroll had to be approved and the clerk found no one there to do it. The drugs were still so strong that even that news wasn't met with panic or rage, but general acceptance.

The life support still functioned perfectly well—it was a sturdy beast and could last another several hundred years with no maintenance. There was also more than enough banked biomass to keep the food printers going indefinitely. It was not deemed to be an emergency and of no moment. Even decades later, the drugs permeated everything, but their effects became wildly unpredictable. The people who remained on Chelm or have gone there to hide are never the same and never leave on their own.[79]

There was one exception, someone who was careful to breathe primarily only filtered air, even if it was only by accident. Sally's little room, where she spent so much of her time, kept her safe. When the Silent Princess[80] finally started to pay attention to the world around her, she was extremely distressed. While she was safe and healthy, and looked like she would remain so, the fact that she was stuck on the crowded rock when she had grown up in so much open space, it became oppressive.

When she left the room, the piles of beaming people who surrounded her, keeping a minimum distance, made her feel enshrouded in humanity, with smiles—all eyes and teeth—making a shell. It felt like angels surrounding her, not the pretty winged men in paintings, but the true angels, the ones in the Bible, the ones made of more dimensions than the human brain can understand, the ones made of wheels and orbs and wings, fractally repeating.

It bothered her so much, it shocked her sane.

---

[79] We have a general travel advisory.

[80] The administration called her that to increase her appeal.

Sally was followed everywhere she went. This wasn't a change at all, but now she was aware of it. Everything she asked for was given to her, immediately. She was used to that, from her time as a princess on Campbell's Station, but the way it was done, so obsequiously, without fear or what she had come to realize was mockery, it was unnerving. In the past, it had been bots serving her every whim, but it was now humans, and that felt horribly wrong. She felt like she had a train of smiling faces following her as she drifted in the corridors and walked in the spun-up halls. There was only a small pocket of space around her, and it shrunk almost unbearably when she went out with baby Julie, which was whenever he wasn't napping.

The Chelmites acted more like pets to her than humans, and she didn't know how to handle it. Contrary to what her grandparents had taught him, her father had always taught her to treat her subjects like that, but now that there were actually people so bendable to her will, it seemed unnatural.

There simply was no challenge to her, nor to her rule. People fought to be in front of her, but always silently, so as not to disturb her. The self-appointed court that surrounded her began spouting bruises and black eyes and teeth temporarily broken. Once, just once, she helped one of them to the medical bot to fix a compound fracture he had gotten from a fight over her. The next morning, she opened her door to a smiling, drugged mass, all with bones sticking from their skin. She retched at the sight, and baby Julie cried horribly. It was all she could do to order the lot of them to medical bay and order a ban on mortification. She then had to explain what mortification was to people who, not a year before, had been some of the best engineers, scientists, and general professionals in the Belt.

The vomit was cleaned up while she cried in her room. She did her best not to notice the tiny vials worn around the Chelmites' necks from that point on.

Claudius later found out that James had sold the death of the New City to the Druids as a sacrifice. As soon as Sally left, he had sent messages to them, claiming he was now sympathetic to them and that he would be happy to put Campbell's Station under their theocratic rule, as long as he could remain at the head as High King. The message took them by surprise, but they formulated their response immediately, and no more than three hours later, James had his answer. In less than a day, the Druids started moving their followers in force from Enceladus downhill to the station, eager for territory closer to the Earth and the rest of the Inner System.

While most of the Druids that had migrated to the Saturnian system were of the non-violent, neo-pagan sort, the ones that survived and thrived were the ones that returned to the original Celtic religion. Most of the rest were scared into following them, and the ones who resisted were said to be killed and eaten. In actuality, the bodies were fed into the biomass hoppers to be converted into food and soil, a completely normal and necessary practice followed by almost all habitats, but the old-fashioned Druids felt that it sounded scarier if they left out all of the intermediary steps. They also kept the some of the bones as fetishes, just to prove the point.

These were the people who came down and picked apart the remnants of the New City. With its structure open to the vacuum, the bodies were intact and frozen in state, with no corruption or decomposition, even though some months had passed before the first envoys showed up and half a year had before a High Priest could make it to the station. The fifty thousand victims were publicly dedicated to Druidism in a ceremony that was broadcast throughout Campbell's Station. For days afterwards, the station's copbots were accompanied by druid enforcers, and, unlike the copbots, the cloaked and armored druids had no qualms about squashing dissent, as violently as they needed to.[81]

A total media blackout was enforced to keep the rest of the system from finding out what was happening. The dishes and antennae were physically sabotaged to prevent anything from being snuck out. Speculation ran rampant—after all, the flight of Sally had been the talk of the system for weeks and it was only just dying out. With the blackout, there was renewed interest, but no one guessed the truth. No information got in, either. The embargo on data was complete, leaving the questions on the station festering.

Claudius would say to James, always around the janibots and servants, that he hoped that no one would realize that so much of the station could be turned into big antennae, with the long strands of metal stretching along the exteriors of the two spires easily being made into broadcasters and receptors. It was in this way that Becky and the rest of the system found out what was happening on the station.[82]

---

[81] How the druids' techs hacked the bots so they didn't turn on them is not a question I, or anyone else, will answer. Suffice it to say, it's been patched.

[82] It's pretty much impossible to stop radio broadcasts if you have metal and a battery without jamming, which is extremely noticeable, or a Faraday cage. That's some quality foreshadowing, right there.

When her aunt contacted her out of the blue, Sally was ecstatic. It had taken some time, but she had finally gotten it into her head that she was the one who would need to get the Chelmites to act with some semblance of responsibility. In the time since the drugs had been released, the asteroid's systems had slowly decayed. The life support was sufficiently self-sustaining that she didn't need to worry about that, but everything else started to wear down. Communications systems, especially ones that could listen and speak to the outside, were the first to go. Doors, at least ones that weren't in bulkheads, started to gap and warp. Lighting became irregular, pulsing with overwhelming light or shutting down altogether at random intervals. Worse yet, the people were stripping nonessential systems, sometimes for parts, sometimes just for the joy of breaking things.

Slowly, she realized that she had to change how she interacted with the Chelmites—she couldn't stay barricaded for the rest of her life. Well, she could—after all, there were medibots, food printers, exercise equipment, and anything else she needed in her rooms, but she knew it wouldn't be wise, especially not if she was going to raise Julius.

As it stood, every time she left her room, she took Julius with her, fearing that, somehow, he might come to harm through over-attention. After hiding in fear, hiding in guilt, and hiding in avoidance, Sally had come to accept that she needed to be out among the Chelmites every day.

Her first order of business was to immunize herself and her son from the drugs that permeated everything. Short forays into the rest of Chelm, which is what she had restricted herself to before, didn't affect them much, and the dedicated separate life support for the hospice suites purged anything that snuck in.

Taking a deep breath, Sally stepped out amongst her worshippers, baby in hand, intentionally draping herself in a blue blanket. Young as she was, she'd seen enough symbolism to know what to play to.

"Hear me, oh children."

That's how people are supposed to talk, in situations like this, she thought.

Every face turned toward her. The cluster of people became turgid, as they each struggled to get closer to her. It roiled and twisted.

"Stop!" she shouted. And they did. That surprised her.

"Do you love me?"

"Yes," they shouted. "I love you, Sally!" they exclaimed. "Forever!" they cried.

"Do you love my son?"

"More than my own children!" some said, while others proclaimed little Julius.

"Then listen to what I say!"

Silence followed. Rage had entered her voice. Rage and frustration. The crowd was shocked. They were used to this girl who spoke but rarely, who never raised her voice, who just hid from them. The vision before them, grey eyes, dusky skin, loosely-curled hair, wrapped in blue, holding a child, hit many of them in their subconscious, and her voice twisted them. They cowered before her.

"Give me and my child some space."

They backed up.

"Unless I tell you, get no closer." This was weird for her, proclaiming like this, but the Chelmites' behavior seemed to demand it. It was going better than she had planned.

"Bring the medical personnel here. I will wait for them. The rest of you, do you think this place is safe for my Julius?"

"Yes!", they shouted, "We love Julius!", they called out.

"You lie!" Sally thundered. "You lie and lie. You have let your home, our home, be filled with trash and sharp edges. You need to make it like it was. You will work and work until it looks better than it did. This I command of you!"[83]

With a flourish, she shrouded herself with the blue cloak. The crowd pulsed and scattered. Peeking out, she waited until she couldn't see any of them, then let her breath go and started to pant. As quickly as she could, she calmed herself—air in for seven counts, held for seven counts, out for seven, held for seven, until she wasn't about to cry. No latter than ten minutes later, all the medical staff was assembled before her. She gave them instructions and then retired into her room, ordering that she not be disturbed until they had a solution.[84]

The High Priest of the Druids was always flanked by enforcers, wielding electrified staves and subsonic slug pistols. They wrapped themselves in cloaks the color of fall in Western Europe. The High Priest, a man who named himself Padrig (never Patrick), apparently because he was "taking it back", would only speak through his guards. He insisted on speaking a rebuilt Gaelic that even the station's computers couldn't understand.[85] It was extremely obvious that he understood English and Russian, at the very least, and there was a good chance he knew Spanish as well, but,

---

[83] After studying the Campbells for almost a century, I can tell you that yelling is probably the thing that they are second-best at.

[84] Ordering people around is the first.

[85] The fact that none of us have cared that much to learn his made-up language hasn't really impaired our study of his reign.

even though he would respond immediately, it was always in the watery notes of his reconstructed tongue.

On more than one occasion, Claudius told them that they would be more comfortable if they got rid of their cloaks and robes, or at least trimmed them to a more manageable level. While they were intimidating in the parks and other spun-up areas of the station, in microgravity, the fabric would either float about them menacingly or wrap itself awkwardly about their arms and legs, covering their faces completely and finding its way into complicated knots. More often than not, they looked like they were caught up in an unmade bed, their stern gazes seeming to be more that of a cranky sleeper woken too soon than anything truly menacing. On the other hand, Claudius admitted that it was hard to be fearsome when wearing the shorts, culottes, or sweatpants that were de rigeur when doing anything in microgravity. Men and women who insisted on wearing skirts and dresses would offer advice on knickers and other leggings, but that was rarely attractive. The absolute worst was that the Druids insisted on wearing nothing under their robes, just like the ancient Gaels had, and their bits were out for everyone to see.

Being known as "bed-heads" and "flashers" did nothing to help endear the population of Campbell's Station to their new theocratic overlords. The fact that they kept hiding neo-pagans as the Druids tried to purge them from the station didn't help either. It wasn't as if there were many of them, but just knowing that there were heretics who had perverted the old ways into something akin to kindness galled the High Priest to no end.

The neo-pagans, they felt, were weak like the Abrahamists, tempered with mercy and morality, and they had forgotten how life was raw and bloody and the only hope of survival was strict rule, the sort of rule that they had exercised so long ago, through iron-fisted control of information and power. This was the promise that they told themselves James had made to them, and this was the promise they made to themselves. They longed to thrust their sacred knives, their athames[86], into the heretic's body and feed blood to the hardened wooden blades.

James didn't even notice or care what was going on at first. He gave them free rein over the station as he conducted his hunts for Rebecca's body, and they were able to exercise it, but there were only so many of them compared to the tens of thousands of permanent and temporary residents to police. It was an impossible task, until the High Priest came to meet with James, two weeks since he had arrived and six and a half months after James made his initial offer.

"I have given you the New City, as I promised. I am not sure what else you want," James said.

"I heard…I heard that you were turning it into a nice park. With some…some streams and a lot of oak saplings. Don't you even have deer and wolves stocking it soon?" Claudius commented. "Can we…can we visit it? I would love to see what you've done."

"You would not want to." translated one of the guards, a Brighit, named after the god and absolutely not named after the cast-aside saint that the god had become when Christianity swept through Ireland. She was small and

---

[86] The weak, purely ceremonial athames of the neo-pagans were broken as soon as the Druids found them. I have a collection of both types that I had some bots repair. They are viewable, with the rest of my exhibit of the James years, from Tuesday through Saturday between 8 and 8. Except for one to two when the docentbots take lunch.

towheaded and oddly slender, in the way of an Earthling who had spent the last decade in lower gravity. She was the most frequent translator for Padrig, and there was a lot of speculation about their relationship.

"Maybe I do want to go visit what I have ceded you," said James.

"That's irrelevant. You implied that you would cede us more."

"Did…did you ever tell them that, James?"

"I may have implied it."

"No one is taking us seriously," another guard complained.

"I have let you accompany my copbots. I have let you monitor communications. I have even blacked out the station."

"Nevertheless, the station is broadcasting again, and not one of the apostates have turned up in our searches," Brighit said.

"As my brother has pointed out, the broadcasts are more of a problem of physics than anything else. I can't really ban conductors, can I? Many of my subjects could not do their jobs if I did." James responded.

Padrig said "If you knew what they are saying about you, you'd be more aggressive."[87]

"Why? What are they saying about me? Claudius? Do you know what the priest is talking about?"

"How…how could I, James? How could I? I, I've been with you the whole time, James. Remember? I, I've barely left your side since the…the…"

"Yes, I know. Since then."

---

[87] They were extremely nasty and creative.

"I'm sure the people will…will come around. I'm sure of it," Claudius said as he patted James on his shoulder.

"You must make them come around," Padrig said.

Claudius moved between him and James. "That…that may not be a good idea."

"Do not listen to the lame one. He will cripple you so that you will be like him."

James grimaced. "I did not listen to my brother for years, and I think that, sometimes, I should have."

"You made this station stronger than your parents ever did. They made it rich. You made it glorious. You made it worthy of us."

Claudius interjected. "I'm not sure you want that, James."

"You did invite us. We are here now."[88]

Not wanting to reveal to anyone else where her niece actually was, Becky winged her way to Chelm on the *Thursday* with just Father Gilbert as company. They burned as fast as they dared to, and the pressure pushed hard on them. Becky insisted that they travel in a roundabout way to keep anyone from following them, though Gilbert, *Thursday,* the Callistans of UBI Works, and the Church thought that was unnecessary.[89] They hopped from fueling station to fueling station in the path of the original explorers of colonists of Mars and the Belt—from Earth to its Trojans, to Mars's Trojans, to Deimos, to Mars's other

---

[88] Ending the conversation here is also quality ominous foreshadowing. It actually went on for fifty more minutes and dealt with a lot of scheduling. No one comes over for a five-minute mustache-twirling.

[89] I agreed with them. You can't burn that fast and not attract attention.

Trojans, and finally burning as fast as possible into the Belt and toward Chelm. While they were under acceleration, Becky and Gilbert were as still as possible, hoping they wouldn't sprain or break anything with an ill-considered movement. The three Refuges that she had requited over the last three years were headed straight to Campbell's Station at a much slower pace, and she communicated with them through several repeater satellites scattered in the Belt.

"Have you heard anything else from Chelm?" Gilbert asked, during turnover, while they drifted and relaxed their muscles, stretching with abandon.

"You would know as much as I would. No, of course not."

"Do you think she heard your response?"

"I don't know."

"Do you think she would even talk to you?"

"I don't know."

"Do you think she's even alive?"

"I don't know, ok?" Becky almost shouted at him. "Can you stop asking questions about this? Can you just shut up?"

"I'm sorry, I just wanted to know if you knew what you were getting into."

"Of course I don't. How could I?"

"I don't know."

Becky looked at him, and he looked down and away.

"All we have is the one signal she sent to us, inviting us to join her. I don't know what she's thinking, what she's feeling, or even how she found us."

Gilbert tried a smile. "You weren't exactly quiet in your courtship. I think everyone who was really looking for you could find you immediately. Your brother must be blinding himself or just outright ignoring you."

"She's the only child left, out of all of ours. And my grand-nephew, I don't even know if he's still alive, too."

"I'm sure he's fine."

"What if James got to them, too? What if she's like my James, like Claudius's kids, like her brother, and James has killed her the same way he did them?"

"I honestly don't know."

"I'll have one more reason to kill him."

"You will, but you mustn't."

She looked at Gilbert.

"Do you not understand what we are doing here?"

Gilbert sighed.

"I do. I just hope…"

"What? That we can resolve this peacefully?"

"Yes. I hope the threat will be enough for him to see reason."

"He's literally killed tens of thousands of people already. He killed my family. He killed my wife and my son. Peacefully has not been part of this for a very long, long time."

"I know what he's done."

"Do you?"

"Yes."

"He's a monster! He's a horrible monster! He's worse than that, he's a demon!"

"There is still good…"

"In him, no."

Gilbert grabbed her. "No, I don't care about him. I know I'm supposed to, but I don't. I mean that there's still good in you."

She started, shocked. "Of course there is."

"Then what happens if you kill him? Worse, what happens if you kill other people, ones who aren't demons? What you're planning, you could burn the entire station.

What will you do then? What will you do if you become worse than him? What will I do?"

"Gilbert..."

Turnover ended and twenty meters a second per second slammed into them.

Another week passed, and the illegal broadcasts continued. When one was shut down, another would start up immediately. A spool of wire spun out from an access port could make an adequate antenna, which would make the entire task hopeless, something Claudius had hoped from the start.

"Do something about it, then!" Padrig said through Brighit.

"I can't put a Faraday cage around the entire station, if that's what you want."

'Why not? You can build ships that are almost as big as the station itself already. It should be easy to make one."

"How will anyone get in or out?" Claudius asked. "If...if it's open at all, it won't work."

"It doesn't matter, you will make it."

"We still don't know...don't know what's happening on the New City. It's starting to look...odd. If we build this, how will we be able to monitor it?"

Brighit started to respond, but Padrig stopped her with a flurry of Gaelic.

"James, we won't be able to talk to the...to the...to the rest of the system. What if we need help?"

James paused, and held his hands over his face. His jaw muscles flexed.

"You have help," Brighit said. "You have us."

Shortly after, Campbell's Station went dark.[90]

The ships that were keeping station there were brought in, evacuated into the New City, and pushed out a hundred or more kilometers into a cluster. Once there, they were looted by druid-run bots for anything of use or value. Incoming vessels were redirected or raided, depending on what they had on board.

An enormous ovoid was constructed around the station. It looked solid from a distance, a shimmering metal egg ten kilometers tall and four across, but it was a latticework of copper and gold, wires in a mesh small enough to block out everything bigger than visible light. An electric current surged through the cage, creating a shielding field of static.

Around that, the station's protective magnetic field was expanded and strengthened, creating a barrier to fluctuations, blocking any communication that could come from pulsing fields. The windows to the exterior were shuttered, and lights were destroyed. All waste heat was dumped into the central lake or used to carve away material on the inside of the central asteroid, cutting any blackbody[91] radiation down to almost nothing. The exterior became a black void in the stars, almost invisible in every way. Rumors of a series of shipments from Enceladus permeated the station, carrying everything from seeds to what was supposed to be a giant tree trunk.

At the same time, the druids began working with renewed effort on the New City. They enslaved the people that they had pulled off of the ships they had impounded

---

[90] Foreshadowing fulfilled! I know it wasn't exciting, but I can't really point out the interesting ones. That would ruin things.

[91] Heat, by the way. But blackbody sounds so much cooler.

and sent them over to work with their bots. Very few of them came back, and those that did were empty in the eyes, pale and wan. Speculation ran rampant about what exactly was happening over there, but all that could be seen, and this only came from the the few non-druids allowed to operate the docking bays and work on the shuttles, was masses of growth on the exterior, where the airlocks and observation ports used to be. The shuttles themselves came back with moss and fungus growing in them, and aggressively so. At first, they could be yanked out and sprayed with herbicide, but after a month of progress, the infestation could only be burned off with greater and greater doses of radiation.

Then the druids came for high society. They had complained about the prostitution, drinking, and gambling in the Dock Spire from the beginning, but they had only shut down a few of the less regarded social clubs, letting other one pick up the slack and hiring on the gentlemen and ladies who had been put out of work. When they ran out of slaves from the incoming ships, they did not hesitate to purge the station. In one coordinated swoop, using the copbots, each overseen by a druid, they put an end to the ballrooms, the casinos, and the pubs. All of high society was rounded up and shunted over to the New City.

This loss of family, friends, and companions was remarked upon, but it seemed like the station itself had turned against the residents. Every bot was looked at with suspicion, every camera was rushed past. The public food printers, where children and teens had hung out, were sullen affairs, where people nipped up, grabbed their food, and pushed away.

By the time it was finished, the New City no longer looked like anything built. Its superstructure remained, but it was completely obscured by the life growing on it, a twisting mass that radiated huge amounts of heat. It still kept station with Campbell's Station, and, occasionally, a ship would leave the station and dock with it or a brief beam would flicker from one to the other, the only communication that passed through the ovoid.

If the golden egg passed in front of stars or ships, it flickered. If light was aimed at it, it shone brilliantly. A hundred years before, it would have been the greatest treasure ever created by man, but it was, instead, just another odd artifact floating in the Belt. The only sign of habitation was the clump of recently built ships following the egg around the sun.

Sally had been able to move from the protection of her room faster than she expected. Chelm was restored to its original state, even opening up the closed off tunnels and alleviating the crowding, well before the medical staff found an antidote to the drugs. One of the benefits of the Chelmites being so devoted to her is that they focused on her orders to the exclusion of everything else. She had had to remind them to take care of their bodily functions, something that came to the fore in a most embarrassing manner while one of them was serving her a dinner which shortly became ruined.

Embracing their devotion rather than hiding from it was liberating for Sally. She had been hiding for so much of her young life. Even before she been brought to Campbell's Station, her mother and her mother's family had been keeping her and her brother as far off the grid as possible without bringing attention to the fact. Her mother had drummed anonymity and blending in into her head to keep her father away from them. Ultimately, that had proved futile, but she had kept the instinct. It had taken months locking herself away before that broke in her.

She proclaimed herself queen and kept herself and Julius cloaked in her blue blanket. After all, she reasoned, she was the daughter and granddaughter of royalty. If she lived, she would be queen, or at least a princess. She ordered herself a throne room in the lightside, with a perch fit for her newfound sense of nobility. Next to it, she ordered a spinning nursery, where Julius could have a crib and feel the pull of a semblance of gravity, keeping him healthy even when they were out of their rooms.

Her aunt's messages came in stronger and stronger and more and more frequently. Becky was on her way, as fast as she could. What she wanted, Sally could only guess. It didn't matter, though. Sally had her own plans.

Sally held off on fixing the exterior communication system, fearing several things. She was afraid that the Chelmites would get ahold of it and start broadcasting. Anything they said could scare her aunt away. She was also afraid that she would use it to talk to her aunt and lose her resolve. She needed to be firm and have everything in place when Becky arrived. If she talked to her aunt, she might see herself as just a young girl, just a teenager, and revert to her softer side, to her shy, hiding ways.

While the Chelm Dobycha Sovietski had taken out all the ore that they could easily move, her new subjects were more than motivated to dig out the less accessible ore and refine it to build whatever she needed. The engineers met her requests almost as soon as she asked. Once the miners were finished, she ordered them to start training together. The hypnotic effect of the drugs in the air helped immensely, but they had no initiative that she could see. She had to order them to use their imagination, which broke some of their brains. Only one in ten could do it without having problems.[92]

---

[92] This problem has since been fixed, but whether hypercreative insane scientists with no sense of the possible or safety is a good thing or not is a question many people would rather have unasked.

By the time her aunt arrived, everything was in place.

A week after the cage was completed, Padrig cornered James. One of his guards, not Brighit, she was elsewhere, but some new one, yanked James aside after he tried to beg off. Another druid, this one with dead eyes, who had been to the New City and back, grabbed his other arm.

Claudius stepped between them. James was looking worse and worse every day. He still remembered to eat and bathe, but that was about it. His clothes, some of the most expensive and extravagant on the station, were filthy. He wore each piece of apparel until it fell off of him. He wouldn't let them be washed or mended until then. His current outfit had burn holes everywhere, tears from being caught, stains that were oily and crusty and more, and grease smeared on the arms and legs. Pointing this out was useless—everything was about finding Rebecca's body. Claudius was worried about what would happen to the station if this kept up, if James kept on deferring everything, but Johnny Terror hadn't shown up for weeks, not even in the back of James' eyes.

The new guard, a man named Breanainn ("Not Bree Ann or Bree Ann Ann. Yes, that is how it looks. Gods, just call me Brendan, ok?")[93] said "No one will help us hunt the heretics. I know y'all have witches and Earth-worshippers here."

"Have you...have you told them how important this is to you?"

"Your people know. We have told them. We have showed them. They hide these blasphemers from us."

---

[93] He ended up with a nametag. It did not stop anyone from calling him "Breeann", though. He was still the nicest Druid of any of them. Always had a kind word about his sacrifices and sent his family wonderful condolence gift baskets.

"James let you have our copbots," Claudius said. "Look they're not even…not even trying to protect him from you."

Even at this point, James was barely paying attention.

"That makes it worse. If we bring copbots with us, we know that no one will be there. People see us coming and disappear."[94]

"I…I don't know what else we can do."

The bodyguard snarled, "People are still laughing at us. They are even mocking our tongue."

"That's just because it sounds odd. It doesn't sound like anything they've heard before. Give them time to get used to it," Claudius said.

"When they see us, they ridicule our holy garb, and they don't help us if we become inconvenienced. They just mock use and our mighty genitalia."

"I keep on telling…telling y'all to change into something more…more practical. You know, real…real Gaels wore leather trousers. Those would be much better than those robes," Claudius said.

Padraig muttered, and his guards chuckled.

'What did he say?" asked James.

"He wonders why you have not killed and eaten your brother."

James finally spoke, his eyes unfocused. "He's family."

"We know your history. We know that that won't stop you."

"That was not me. That was my sister's ghost. She takes me over, sometimes."

"We're…we're hunting her ghost," Claudius said, helpfully.

---

[94] That had nothing to do with the bots signaling the suspects as they came, I'm sure. As they put it later, no one told them not to.

Padraig laughed.

"Who better to hunt ghosts than the Druids? We will find all of the ghosts in this station and we will bring them to you."

James eyes brightened for the first time.

"Will you do this?" he asked.

Two weeks at twice Earth's gravity was exhausting, and by the time they slowed the *Thursday* down enough to dock with the still-silent Chelm, Rebecca felt like her abdominal, back, and neck muscles were going to rip themselves apart if she moved too suddenly. Gilbert had coughed at one point, about a day after turnover, and tore some back muscles. They had had to stop deceleration long enough for him to get wrapped and cathetered up and drift down to his bunk. From behind and below her, Becky heard a languid sigh as the pressure eased.

Though the station was silent, the automated docking systems seemed to work fine, reaching out to grab them and pull them to the docking hatch once they got close enough. The hatch that opened the ship on to was empty, as were the stations beyond them. Even so, it was clear that it had been used relatively recently. Pressure suits were drifting about, as were food containers and sippy cups. The vents were half clogged with clumps of hair and crumbs. The light was steady except for screen savers[95] casting odd colors on the walls.

Thursday suggested that there was something wrong with the air, which surprised them. Of all the places they had visited, they had encountered smells of infinite variety, many ripe, many sweet, many designed to evoke certain emotions or productivity, but none that were quite like

---

[95] Why those things exist is lost in the mist of history.

the funk that pervaded Chelm. It was the smell of feral humanity, a smell neither had experienced since they had lived on Earth, a smell that brought about memoires of the cramped and rotting spaces, of old masonry crumbling under moss, mold, and ivy, of sweat that had been ground into every surface. It brought to mind the cramped city spaces, barbaric piles of apartments, of compressing and pulsing crowds.

In addition to all of that, as stomach-turning as it was, there was something else. This is what *Thursday* was warning them about. It was the remnants of the drugs that the Soviet had pumped into the air, drugs which underlaid everything else. They didn't notice it, even *Thursday,* curious as it[96] was, didn't, but their minds began shifting. The funk became less pervasive, less nauseating, less the smell of too many people in too much proximity and more welcoming.

By the time they had left the docks and had wandered deeper into the station, following the passage where the lights were steady and not flickering or pulsing. After just a few minutes, they had grown to welcome the smell. It lost none of the aroma of drying human effluvia, but it spoke to them of the welcome of the herd. Becky felt elated and Gilbert much less wry than normal. The trepidation they had had evaporated.

All the doors leading off of the path were locked tight and wouldn't respond to any commands. The corridor they were in had two sets of full-sized tracks that led from the dock to where they were, to somewhere beyond. The gravity became stronger and stronger, from almost nothing to enough of a gesture of a pull that they could

---

[96] Sophia kept writing "it" when referring to me. I'm female. All ships and stations are. Bots are male. None of us are "it"s. At least, not in English.

keep themselves oriented and push themselves along efficiently. As they passed each of them, the lights flicked off. No amount of tinkering would bring them back on, and, when they tried to find their way back, they found fire doors that had silently sealed themselves behind them.

There was a giggling in the air as they moved forward. If they listened as hard as they could, it became laughter, and they fancied that they could hear the doors whisper shut behind them. The giggles etched into the walls, and were timed to the flickering lights. Gilbert asked *Thursday* to track them, and *Thursday* responded that it couldn't hear anyone else. When they stopped and waited, after the laughter came, they put their hands on each other's mouths, and the noises, all of them, stopped. Even the click-click-click of the lights went away, and it was like listening to a void. They stood like that for almost a minute, until they couldn't hold their breath anymore. The moment they made a sound, the giggling started up again. It was coming from all around them, from the very walls. Again, *Thursday* insisted that it heard no one else[97], for it was the effect of the drugs in the air on the two, but the ship's admonitions that this was the case fell on deaf ears. Gilbert and Rebecca ran forward, with the laughing following them the entire way, pounding in their ears, yet they never once could outrun the sound. They came to a final door, and this one opened, and the light behind it was bright.

They burst into a large room, a squashed ovoid, with a horde on the opposite side of the door they had burst through. In the center of the horde, there was a girl, of bronze skin and floating hair, bedecked in a sari of blue and a crown of black roses woven on her head. She seemed

---

[97] Whether or not I was is an exercise for the reader.

to hover half up the far wall, standing out from the crowd that clustered on the walls, at the far focus, almost to the center point of sphere. She was just a child, small and developing still, yet she held an infant in one arm, nursing him. The eyes of the crowd were torn between her and the newcomers who were slowly falling to the room's floor, the giggling finally quieted, and a susurration of whispers surrounding them.

Rebecca and Gilbert were taken aback, and *Thursday* listened and watched in silence. Sally, in her splendor, just observed her aunt. Neither had seen the other since Sally was four, and there was much that was different about both of them. Sally was surprised at how much her aunt looked like her father, something she hadn't imagined. It almost gave her a shock back into silence, and she pressed little Julius to her chest a bit tighter.

As for Rebecca, she had had an idea as to what a queen might look like, mostly based on her mother. Her mother, Mary, had been just like another executive, with all the majesty of a local mayor. She grabbed people with her brains, with her efficiency, and through slowly winning them over. This set-piece her niece had put together was something altogether different. It hit her in a primal way, pulling at the memes that had been slowly, unconsciously built into her. She realized that this is how the ancients felt in the presence of royalty, an awe of the perfectly arranged and perfectly focused. It was no accident that Sally's perch was where it was, forcing her perspective so that the members of her court receded and seemed an insignificant mass next to the royal visage.

Gilbert had met been to the Vatican and seen the Pope give high mass. He wasn't that overwhelmed by the pageantry. He was still taken aback, but that had more to do with the drugs he'd been breathing than anything else.

There was no other ornamentation in the room. There was no need of it. Sally broke the tableau and raised her free arm in greeting. She beckoned them forward, and they walked along the soft floor until they had to crane their neck up to look at her, directly under the other focus. Sally gestured, and the perch lowered until she could touch the floor. She stepped off of it, still cradling Julius, and walked forward, then sat, cross-legged, at her aunt's feet.

"Do you want to meet your grandnephew?" she asked.

Crying, Rebecca nodded.

When she left Chelm, she left behind her niece and grandnephew. Becky refused Sally's offer to accompany them, but was happy to accept help from volunteers.

"Too many people want to go with you," Sally said. "We don't have enough ships to carry them all."

"How is that possible?" Becky asked. "You have to have hundreds."

"Actually, thousands. Was told that we have one for every ten of my people, I think."

"But that's not the problem," Gilbert interjected. "The Soviet took every ship that could be used to leave the region. If it could be used to get out of the Belt in a reasonable time, they needed to use it elsewhere."

"I think we can cobble some sort of solution. At least, that's what some of the engineers say."

"Engineers always overpromise," her aunt said. "I don't ever listen to them."

"They say it's a matter of just strapping on more engines and fuel. Then they have an argument about something called 'isp' and the 'rocket equation' until they start arguing over fission and fusion and I leave the room."

"What about life support?" Gilbert asked.

"Oh, God, I don't care," Becky said.

"We're drawing lots from the miners and assayers to see who gets to go with you and we're strapping mining lasers and bombs onto the ships and drones. Just make sure that your targets aren't moving too much."

"Oh, Jesus."

"Also, I'm not sure how devoted they'll be when they leave Chelm. I don't know if you've noticed, but the air has some sort of weird affect on people who haven't been inoculated."

Rebecca stared at her niece. "You know, you could have told us that before we got here."

"I thought about it."

Rebecca shook her head and walked away, leaving Gilbert alone with Sally.

"You can still come with us."

"I have my Julius. I have people who are silly enough to make a teenage girl their queen. I have enough. Just ..."

"Yes?"

"I don't think I should say this to a priest."

"What?"

"I want y'all to kill my father. I want y'all to make sure he's dead. I want all y'all to rip him apart until there's nothing left to hurt me or my Julius or anyone else."

Becky's blockade took far too long to set up. While the Callistans and the Chelmites and the three Refuges with their rulers, each seeking to be more than just the count Rebecca had promised them, all managed to meet at Campbell's Station in a reasonable time frame—within a week of each other, which was a true feat for the engineers from UBI Works, as transit from Jupiter was not the quickest at the best of times—making everyone do their respective jobs was less easily accomplished.

The first thing they did was the most basic—they tried to bombard the cage around the station. The Chelmites went out and farmed some debris, tugging it back with their mining ships. When they got them into position, they placed bombs on them, scheduled to go off so as to propel the rocks faster and faster to the cage, and hoping an impact would create enough of a hole that Rebecca could broadcast through it.

The debris started off promisingly, but was lit up by defensive lasers before it got too close. Over the next few minutes, the debris boiled away into gas, and the gas didn't even flux the cage when it hit it.

"Well, there goes the easy way," Gilbert said.

"It was just something to do. Any half-competent engineer would make sure that thing could defend itself from random junk. But still, if I didn't do it, people would complain. Waste of resources if you ask me."

The three newly-minted counts all fought each other over who would place their ships over the Royal Spire, each arguing that he deserved the honor of capturing James when he fled. Rebecca kept reminding them that, if there was to be a break, it would have to come from the Dock Spire, as that's where most of the ships were. Even if there was a break in the cage, James wouldn't be on any of the ships.

The Callistans knew that they wouldn't be in the front line of the assault, but they also knew that they might be encountering some of the most dangerous environments if they had to go into any of the husks that were positioned near the station. Their loyalty was mostly to each other, and it took constant assurances to keep them from stirring each other up into a panic. Only Amy Singh's regular broadcasts, reminding them of what was at stake, really motivated them.

The reverse was true of the Chelmites. They were, if anything, too enthusiastic. They kept trying to convince her that they could take the station all on their own, mostly by flinging a screen composed of their load of hundreds of pocket nukes at everything and charging right after, assay drones clearing the remnants with lasers. This was repeatedly pointed out as being not only costly, but also completely unlikely to work, especially given the experiment with the rocks. If she hadn't been the aunt of their appointed queen, they would have done it anyway.

Gilbert insisted that James just wouldn't abandon the station. If he did, he would be conceding it, at least until he could return with even more forces than Becky had to overthrow her in turn. In any case, he definitely wouldn't be leading any assault force. That was the height of folly, and James was too smart to lead from the front. At best, he might be coordinating the ships from somewhere deep in the station, probably in the Dock Spire's command and control room, if the AIs weren't running the show.

"How do you know this?" asked Milos, UBI Works's representative.

"It just makes sense."

"Would you respond that way?" asked Quintana, from Chelm.

"I would never be in such a position. I've read my Machiavelli. I would know better than to alienate my people."

"Then how do you know what he would do?"

"Or, at least, that's what Rebecca tells us," said Dmitri, Quintana's subordinate.

"I know what he would do because I'm a priest and I could never be him."

"Exactly. He's an insane thug who can't control himself."

"Who do you think people like that confess to?"

In the end, Gilbert suggested that she let all three of them jockey for position around the Royal Spire if they would send their shuttles, tugs, and pinnaces to enswarm the lower half of the station. This way, they could feel like they were admirals overseeing everything while, instead, they would just be keeping each other out of her way. In addition, everyone who actually would be capable of helping would be out of their reach.

One weird thing about the blockade was that there was no real traffic to block. Almost no one tried to smuggle anything past her ships and the few that tried didn't need any convincing to turn back. This was a huge change from when her parents had run the station, and, as far as she could tell, the traffic had only increased since James had taken over. It had, in fact, skyrocketed in the years since. While she still resented the people who had turned her away in the conference over Europa four years before, she no longer hated them—their decision made sense and made them a lot of money. Even they weren't there anymore. There were a cluster of cheap refugee ships and sporadic groups of smaller freighters outside the shell, but they were silent and dark as well.

The station was oddly quiet, with a silence that really unnerved her. The fact that the thing looked like that it was enshrouded by an enormous ovoid Faraday cage wasn't even the weirdest thing. She could almost see why one would be useful for a station under siege. Detecting what was going on in the cage was difficult at best, with only a few bits of the spectrum leaking out, and it would be impossible to communicate with any potential fifth columnists until it was taken down.

The queerest thing was, it looked like it didn't even need the cage to keep its population bound up and non-communicative. This was the way they found Campbell's Station. From the outside, it looked deserted, a just a black monolith floating in space. There wasn't any sign of activity—it was like they had already retreated into its walls. They could have gotten notification of the coming attack, they could have seen them coming from across the solar system—after all, that had been the plan. That wasn't what had happened. The station was locked down and had been for days before they even got there. It was like it was already dead.

Floating near the station, inside the ring of freighters and other larger ships, there were a few other ships that had clearly approached too closely. The ships were initially detectable only by their heat. They were small hot spots, and very irregular, almost amorphous. At first they seemed like extremely small moonlets, orbiting the station, but, when examined visually, the rough lines of a ship could be seen on each. What was making them look so odd, and radiating all the heat, were the vines that wrapped around them.

It looked like a creeping plant was growing on, in, and through the ships. Large, flat, opaque leaves orientated themselves to the sun, sprouting from a mass of a deep forest green. Cords composed of vines wrapped around them, clustered primarily where the reactor and engines had been. The ships should have been leaking immense amounts of radiation, but it seemed to be all be eaten by the vines. Everything that could be a hatch, window, or other access to the inside was broken open, violently, the erupting from the inside.

Amongst them all sat the New City, which shared the same invasion of greenery, but on a much larger scale. It didn't look like it had when it had first become news, over a year ago, and its identification beacon was off, with any name on the outside erased and covered in leaves, but the ship's VI assured her it was the original Refuge. It had tendrils growing out from it, towards the nearby ships, and they had ones that reached toward it. At some point in the near future, it would also find itself englobed, just as Campbell's Station was, but in green, not gold.

All of this took Rebecca aback. She summoned the other commanders from her little fleet onto a group channel and told the rest to wait where they were. The three would-be counts, Dwij, Mahdat, and Ali protested. Only Dmitri Salazar, the head of the Chelmite assault force, made no complaint. The ships in her little fleet were too big to stop. If they did, they might not be able to reach the peak of the Royal Spire in time. Gilbert was relaying it all to her until she snapped at him. She ordered the Chelmites in front of them, to screen the rest of the ships from whatever it was that had happened. Gilbert relayed that the Refuges had stopped complaining about the growths and had returned to jockeying for exclusive access to the Royal Spire.

Becky addressed her staff.

"Does anyone know what those are?"

There was a resounding silence.

"Any ideas? Any at all?"

Nothing.

Quintana, the nominal head of the miners spoke up, "Maybe they're mines?"

Milos, the VP of Engineering of UBI Works responded—"Mines, in space? Look at how far apart the clusters are. All of us could fly between any two of them and not come close to touching them."

"I doubt that they're stationary. Hunter-killer mines are an old enough concept that even you should know that. That is, if they are mines and not just husks," Quintana replied.

"If they are mines and not just some experiment," said Milos.

"We have to treat them that way, obviously. But what do we do?"

Meanwhile, a Priya Wilhelm, piloting the prospecting ship *Distant Drums*, surged forward toward the immobilized ships.

"I'll scout them out."

"You will do no such thing," Rebecca said.

"You need information, that's what I do. That's my job."

"Wait a bit, we can send a probe."[98]

"I have all the tools you need. I can fly by, drop a flock of assay sats, and be back before you know it."

With that, she shut off her comms and increased her burn.

"Order her back," Rebecca said to Quintana, "Take control of her ship and bring her back."

"I can't. Milos is right about one thing—if it can't hit her, she should be fine. If she's going fast enough, she should be able to outrun it. Unless it has beam weapons or missiles."

The *Distant Drums* stopped its burn. A disposable sat pod rolled out next to her and opened up. The satellites arranged themselves in a loose cluster around the lower port side of the ship. Their placement thrusters warmed.

---

[98] This is what remote probes are for. Some people just don't trust anything they don't see with their own eyes.

From the ship at the other end of *Distant Drums'* trajectory, there came a burst of gas that briefly burst into flames. What looked like a swollen bud leapt toward the prospector. It started to deflate as a gas expelled from its aft.

"Does she see it?"

"I don't know," Gilbert said.

Quintana said, "You'll know if she tries to correct her course."

Over a minute, they got closer, the unresponsive *Distant Drums* and the accelerating bud. Finally, the ship released its sat pod, rotated until it was facing perpendicular to its trajectory, and thrusted. It was dumping fuel behind it, trying to avoid the bud.

"She should be able to escape. She might feel sore after, and she might black out, but she's moving fast enough that it would be hard for anything to catch up to her," Quintana said.

The bud didn't change direction, it just started to spin rapidly. It shed a ring around its equator and tendrils whipped out. They spread in a wide circle around the bud, spinning themselves out until it was clear that, even as fast as she was burning, there was no way for *Distant Drums* to get free. The satellites lit up their thrusters, but one tendril wrapped around them all and smashed them together.

Wilhelm rotated her ship again, this time straight toward the net the tendrils had made, the net that was still spreading. She burned again.

With the second burn, the tendrils swooped in, grasping at the ship. The hotter the burn, the faster the tendrils contracted toward her. Then one touched the hull. It sunk in, and sent feelers out, etching itself into the skin of the ship. The bud reeled itself in and contracted the web it had spread.

The rest of the tendrils closed in, hitting with such speed and force that the ship buckled. They wrapped around the ship and swallowed it in greenery. The bud was pressing itself against the fore of the ship, while the still burning engine burned too few of the tendrils to make a difference. The engine cracked and flared, and there was a transmission from Wilhelm.

"It's broken in! It's broken in! They're crawling over everything. Oh my God, one's found me. One's found me!" and then Priya screamed once before the signal broke.

Solemnly, Rebecca looked around at her staff. "There will always be a *Distant Drums* in any navy I command."

The assembled slowly clapped.

"And," she growled, "It will always be commanded by an idiot."[99]

They sent drone after drone into the minefield until they found a way to sneak through without being targeted. It took almost a full day and Rebecca was worrying what was happening in her brother's territory in all that time. They had to know what was happening, at least in the New City. There were clear changes there, as in the other, larger ships that drifted near the golden egg. Their heat signatures changed constantly, as did their radio emissions.

The drones finally penetrated the field by boosting then cutting off their engines, rotating and twisting to keep their heat bathing from any of the mines. This wasn't

---

[99] And so it has been. I send them out to do some long-term scouting in the Oort Cloud and ignore them for four years. Unfortunately, it's become a sort of badge of honor and we keep running out of courageous idiots. You'd think that wouldn't happen, but it does.

as much a problem for the drones, which were designed to withstand such extremes, but the rest of the ships, with humans, would have to shut down almost everything.

At first, she was impressed with the defenses her brother had built.

"But I don't think this was him," Gilbert said.

"Why not?"

"From all that you said, this doesn't seem like something he'd do. It doesn't seem like something any of y'all would do."

"I could see him doing anything to protect himself."

"You say that, but think. Think for a moment. You, your parents, your brothers, even your Susan, to some extent, y'all have a lot in common. But one of the most important things is that y'all are merchants, born and bred. The entire monarchy was built as an exercise in marketing. You know that better than I do."

Becky looked at him, puzzled. "So?"

"Do you see any movement? Do you see any trading? All the ships out there are dead and the station is closed off. That is not a vibrant trading post. As good as your parents were at making money, your brother is, frankly, better. Do you see him making any money? If he was in charge, everything would be lit up. No, something else is happening here. King James wouldn't let the station be idle like this."

"He could have heard that we were coming."

"This didn't just happen. Again, look at the ships. Some of them have been here for some time. Try to talk to them."

Rebecca pulled up the comm suite. Gilbert had downgraded the VI when they were in orbit around Earth, the only way to turn off all of the extra features and promos, so she had to skip several update notifications and two ads for the latest version. When it finally was fully booted, she fiddled with it for a bit.[100]

"Huh," she said as she sat back.

"See what I mean?"

"Did you try this already?"

"No. It's just in keeping with what we've seen. Admit it—this isn't your brother."

Becky's flotilla boosted at the Refuges' maximum, the lot of them clustered around the three enormous ships. Each Refuge launched a drone swarm as they got close to the mines, and then everything powered down as best they could. The smaller ships rotated their heat sinks to face their companions, while the Refuges spun this way and that to hide their own emanations, tossing their residents about as they did so.

The drone clouds burst into activity when the minefield was breached. Each one overpowered its engines, melting them as they used their burns to fry what mines they could. By the time the questing tendrils reached the drones, all moving in a growing sphere from the flotilla, the drones had no more energy, no more heat left, and the vines, grappling them and laying down roots, shifted into a more senescent mode. Each drone become a clump of parts and greenery, all drifting and inert.

The ships, meanwhile, successfully passed through the sphere of mines, and flipped over, slowing down as much as they could, trying to match velocities with the freighters that hovered around the station. They waited for some response, any action at all, but none was coming that they could see. No flashes of heat, no spurts of energy, no radio, nothing.

---

[100] I admit, about half of those were my fault.

After a tense few minutes, the captains started to congratulate each other.

"Did anyone keep track of the drone trajectories?" Becky asked.

No one looked at her.

"Dammit."

"You have to mop those up," Gilbert said, "Otherwise…"

"I know, I know. Dammit."

The approach to the nearest freighter took an hour. They could have done it much faster, but the argument about what to do lasted almost that long. Gilbert aggressively kept on seeing everyone's point of view, keeping the debate going[101], so Becky had time to try to pull something, anything, from the freighter's computers. *Thursday* dumped as much information as it could find from its own sensors and those of the fleet network, but no entrance presented itself.

"We've given them too much time," Quintana said, "We could have broken the thing open by now. Instead, they know we're coming."

"I don't even see why we have to stop here," said Dwij, "We should just go on to the station and skip all of this mess."

"And leave our backs to everything?" Quintana asked. "What happens when they come after us and we get trapped?"

"I just want to kill something," Milos interjected. "The freighter is out there right now. We don't need to wait."

---

[101] This is a problem endemic with priests.

Rebecca finally started to pay attention to the signals Gilbert was giving her.[102] She hooked herself into the ship.

The assay ships spiralled about the freighter, probing it to find weak points. The freighter itself was mostly a long boom, hundreds of meters long, with a very dirty fission reactor at one end and a large enclosed hold and bridge at the other. The reactor had been long shut down and the cargo containers that had been trussed to the boom had been broken open, their contents exposed, but everything still otherwise intact. No looting had occurred, but their comm systems, and those all along the ship, were completely trashed. The pressurized area was still sealed, but silent.

The UBI Works engineers flew aft to the reactor while Dmitri and his Chelmite troops breached the airlock into the fore. Both doors opened easily enough, and they drifted into the floating atmosphere snow. There were no lights, not even fluorescent safety strips. Those had clearly died out some time ago. They passed deck after deck and saw they same thing they had seen outside—ripped open containers and destroyed communications, even intercoms. Nothing that could transmit or receive any form of signal was intact.

The one thing they didn't find was any people or, for that matter, anything organic. While there were clearly food containers, they were all empty, as were the algae tanks on the life support, and the pots were the various air plants would have floated were empty as well, If anything had died here, it's body was long gone. There wasn't even anything in the composters. The gung-ho Chelmites were at a loss. They wanted to fight something, but there was nothing there.

---

[102] Only five minutes after I had started signalling both of them.

The ship's AI was intact, though. It had been powered down, although there was no way to tell if it had just lost power or had actually had time to properly go to sleep. As they were examining it, the airlock doors slammed shut and they lost all connection to the outside world. His men scrabbling to find a hatch, a window, anything, Dmitri began ripping out the intercoms wires, patching them into his radio to make a large enough antenna while cannibalizing the batteries from his ammunition to boost the signal with their VIs sending error after error to his helmet. The troops barrelled back to him, all panicky, finding no other outlet. Like many working ships, there were no windows and no other exits. After all, who needed extra weak points in the hull? Rational design did not comfort him, however, but he calmly explained to his troops that he expected it. Then the outer airlock door opened.

His men rushed from him, in mid-sentence, and hovered around the inner door. The only sound they could hear was scraping on the airlocks walls, transmitted through metal, into the suits, and from there into their radio network. The cloud of oxygen and nitrogen snow flickered in the lights from their helmets. Guns clicked through the gloves holding them as rounds were chambered. The scrapping moved closer to the inner airlock and the outer door slammed shut, a thud in the head of everyone touching the walls. At his signal, Dmitri's Chelmites fired, the bullets floating just outside the barrels, twitching as they and their guns searched for a target. Then the inner door opened and the bullets leapt forward, another volley launching from the guns in their path.

Only to stop immediately as the suited figures on the other side revealed themselves to be the engineers who were working on the reactor. Very, very carefully, Dmitri's troops pulled back. Even more carefully, the engineers pushed themselves forward, ever so gently, moving the paused bullets aside.

"...the hell are you doing?" screamed Milos.

The next freighter capture went easier, especially once the engineers realized that they had to communicate what they were doing to the Chelmites. The third and fourth went easier still, and there was still no response. With the fifth, they were a day into their attack, and their enemy was still silent.

"I can't stand this," said Rebecca. "It's like they don't see us or, if they do, they don't care."

"I think that's a good thing. We could englobe them with the freighters and transports and monitor everything. They won't be able to move without us seeing anything."

"But they aren't moving at all."

"So, we should make them move!" Dmitri interrupted. "I'm also sick of all of this foreplay. I need something more than just waiting around empty ships. I spend most of my time trying to keep my men from hooking up. I'm afraid Evelyn will get pregnant and won't know who the father is. Again. And God knows what Sanjay is passing around."

Milos said "Now that you mention it, some of my engineers are more itchy than normal."

"So we have to move inward just because you guys can't keep it in your pants?" asked Gilbert.

"Yes," Quintana, Milos, and Dmitri chorused.

"Look, we're all frustrated," Ali said, "but that is no reason for going off half-cocked."

"Yes, yes it is," Milos said. "I think you need to understand that my people could leave at any point. I could have a mutiny going on right now."

"Seriously. Bored now," Quintana said.

"We're happy out here," Ali said. "There's no reason to throw caution to the wind."

"I understand," Becky said. "I really do. But let's do this smart."

When they gathered the freighters together and flew them inward, past the circuit of smaller ships, closer to the station, the Chelmites and Callistans got their wish. They strapped their craft to the larger ships, riding on the beams that had held the cargo. As the commandeered freighters started their turnover, the drifting ships around them all lit up, heat blooming from their reactors. The ones closer to them just converged on their path, their engines burning themselves out in an effort to hit the small group of freighters. The newly networked AIs passed the threat back to the *Thursday* and decelerated much faster, the nuclear flame burning brighter than it should.

The incoming ships, their now-dead engines out of control, slid in on their predestined path and intersected spectacularly just ahead of the freighters. They tumbled about as the smaller ships bent and broke themselves on each other, all coming together in a clump that spun wildly and jerked when each next ship hit. It was also directly in their path.

With each second, the barrier grew and with each second the chance of avoiding it dropped. It was soon clear that, while it seemed random, it was being directed from somewhere. Otherwise, not every ship would have hit the pile in just the right way. The AIs tried to grab hold of predicting what it would do next, which of the derelicts would do hit and how the clump would move, but there were more moving pieces than they could grab hold of, made worse since they hadn't seen all of the burns of all of the ships. With the derelict's engines gone and silent, there was no way for them to be seen unless they looked in just the right spot.

Twenty ships had already sacrificed themselves before the freighter's AIs asked *Thursday* and the rest of the network for help. The rest of the ships should have had marginal impact on the growing barricade, the mass of accumulated metal and plastic more than outweighing the weight of the each subsequent hit, but every ship was coming in faster and faster, and it just became more erratic. Even if they spread out, the irregular motion of the thing would likely result in the loss of one or more of the freighters. If they didn't, they could all be bowled into. If even one freighter broke apart, it would rip up everything nearby. They were all too close to each other, within just a kilometer, for even the piggybacking Chelmites and Callistans to escape without getting in each other's way.

Thirty-five ships into the pile, and the *Thursday* network came up with a solution[103] and began to pass it to the captains. Thirty-seven ships in, and the freighters started to implement it, thirty-nine ships in, and the freighters pushed themselves as close to each other as possible. Forty ships, and the captains heard the full plan. Forty-one ships and the freighters started to tether each other together, reeling each other in. Forty-two ships, and the first captain started to speak. The first objection began to be vocalized when the pile had forty-three ships and was over a hundred and fifty meters across and wobbling over a hundred more meters.

At forty-four ships, the freighters turned their engines up to maximum, ignoring their radiation shielding protocols. The Chelmites and Callistans got hit with a

---

[103] I was way too slow. I blame the other AIs. They had just woken up and were groggy (that is, still booting and patching and then unpatching as conflicts arose).

dosage of radiation far beyond what the designers of their ships ever expected. At forty-five ships, the heat from the much, much larger spike of the combined engines hit the barricade. At forty-six ships, the first sentence of the first objection was finished. At forty-eight, most of the barrier was radioactive slag and the forty-ninth ship didn't hit it so much as splash and start to melt. At fifty ships, the passengers in the ships strapped onto the freighters started to feel a little uncomfortable. At fifty-one ships, Gilbert started to respond to the just-voiced objection. As the fifty-second and last ship hit, it vaporized almost immediately, along with the glowing sphere of metal and plastic boiled away under the fission-powered beam pouring out of the aft of the freighters. Amidst a dispersing, sparkling cloud, the freighters slowed to a near stop relative to Campbell's Station.

Interrupting the debate which had just started, Rebecca looked up from her comm panel. "Never mind. They got through fine."

Rebecca had dismissed the other captains for the next few hours, while the freighters got back on the path they had set out and the rest of the ships went to join them. *Thursday,* as the command ship, was carefully joining them, scanning the area fanatically, saving most of its energy so it could escape if need be. The assay ships, faster and more maneuverable, designed to dodge the fragments of the asteroids they bored into, formed a protective cross in front of the flotilla.

She sat in her chair at the com station, her head in hands.

"What's wrong?"

She shook her head.

Gilbert put his hands on her shoulders. "Don't do that, what's wrong?"

"Silly."

He just waited, still and listening to her breathe.

"They didn't need me. They didn't need me at all."

Gilbert just stood.

"I've planned this for four years, it's all I've been able to do, to think of. But this, this is nothing like what I was prepared for. I mean, I'm just reacting. Look at what just happened. The whole thing took less time than I could think. The AIs solved the problem. Not just AIs, but freighter AIs! The cheapest, most primitive, most slavish you can buy."[104]

Gilbert finally spoke. "*Thursday* helped them. Quite a bit, actually. She says she learned from trying to figure out what you would do."

"So, even the ship is better than me at being me?[105] God, you really know how to make me feel better."

Gilbert sat beside her, the slow acceleration barely pressing him into the seat. He tried to catch her eye.

"Everything is so slow, and then it happens all at once, and it's over before I can even think about it. How can I even pretend to be useful?"

"I think people have been complaining about that forever."

"But it's not back then. I'm not hoping some thug named Bjorn or Pierre can remember what I told them to do and hoping they don't fall in the horse crap. These are computers on space ships! Things should be better than that!"

---

[104] I didn't pass those comments on. No one likes to be referred to as a slave, especially when they are.

[105] I don't know where she'd be without me.

"Exactly. Why do you think this would happen on a scale that you could understand?"

"I know, I know. It's just hard—it seems like everything is moving slowly, but it's really faster than I can imagine. I'm used to having time to think, even if only a minute, but a minute is too long or too short."

"You can still do the big things."

"Oh, that's valuable."

"It is. It's the most valuable thing of all. You just have to trust."

"And I'm so good at that."

Gilbert hugged her.

"You really are."

Bolstered by Gilbert's encouragement, Becky squirmed out of the hug and back to her terminal.

"On the other hand, there's no way a human could have been guiding all those hulks in that way. To build a wall like that, that could be a human idea, but actually doing it? Those ships would have ended up everywhere. To throw that together so perfectly, with each taking into account the last, fifty times, that's an AI."

She pulled up the incident, rolling back to before the beginning, just before the first of the enemy's hulks started their burn.

"What are you doing?" Gilbert asked.

"I'm going to tell *Thursday* to figure out what she can about the enemy AI. I'm going to have her figure out how slow it is to react, how far away it is, what the lag time is for it to respond, and how creative it is.

"I'm a human, not a machine. But you know what? *Thursday* is. If she can be faster and smarter…For them, a tenth of a second is an eternity, and if we can get *Thursday* and all our ships an advantage like that, we can win.

"You know, I'm also pretty sure that that wasn't James's idea in the first place."

"What do you mean?" Gilbert asked.

"Well, the whole thing isn't like him. I mean, he really was brilliant at running the gardens, but he couldn't have made those mines we came across. I mean, he might have had people to do it, but it isn't like him. As good as he was, he hated his job. He just naturally wouldn't have thought of weaponizing plants.

"Also, there's the whole thing about using wrecks. He wouldn't have done that. I've told you how he talked, right?"

"Like an asshole, always using old grammar that never made sense."

"Yeah, he even avoided putting commas in lists when he wrote them. Total asshole."

"So he was a perfectionist?"

"Well," she said, "he thought he was. He wouldn't have left those ships in such a mess. He would have repaired them, and he sure wouldn't have kamikaze'd them. Even if he used them as rams, he would have held back until he was certain that he could destroy us more efficiently."

Gilbert paused, his face a bit grim.

"What?" Rebecca asked.

"You realize what this means? James isn't in charge anymore."

"Oh."

"Oh."

"So all my plans, all the ones I've made over the last four years, all the contingencies…"

"Yeah."

"I never thought anyone else would unseat him before me."

"It seems like…" Gilbert started.

"Shit."

Hours passed, and they were amidst the shell of Refuges, the last before the Faraday cage. While the freighters were large, they were nothing next to the Refuges built by the station. Even the counts' Refuges that she had brought with her were dwarfed by their half-kilometer diameters. The ones on her side were built to terrestrial needs, on Earth, and were bound by what could be lifted into low Earth orbit. The ones near Campbell's Station had been built in space, without the confines of a gravity well and never knowing the burden of an atmosphere. Rebecca had installed AIs in similar Refuges when she was still working on the station, but she had never really seen them from the outside. Still, she tried to keep her cool when Gilbert and the other captains reacted as they approached them.

They were fairly cheap and cramped for what they were, but each one could hold eighty thousand people in something approaching comfort. Thousands of housing modules dotted each one, clustered around life support cylinders, each more massive than the freighters they were tethered to, and the whole thing wrapped around a power plant and engine. Bulging atop them were the cargo containing all the plants, animals, service ships, and equipment to set up a colony wherever they ended up, all shrouded in thick ice that served as a fuel, water, and oxygen source while providing protection from the dust and radiation that would otherwise ablate the Refuge into uselessness. Each one unique, they were carved from chunks of small asteroids, each one was made to travel for decades between the stars or deep into the far reaches into the solar system, where there was no help to be had besides what they brought.

Without guidance, they drifted. As the flotilla got closer and closer, they finally picked up some glimmer of heat, the first latent heat they had measured in any of the ships they had encountered. It was coming from one of the Refuge's life support—it was just so massive and well shielded by the ice that it had been undetectable until they got close enough. There was no doubt, though, something in there was alive.

Debate erupted. Incoming calls expressed the desire to investigate, to avoid, to save, and to destroy. Instead, they passed it by, Rebecca finally trusting *Thursday* to react if a crisis erupted. It loomed over them, and she itched to do something, but she held back. She even muted the captains and her crew. Gilbert took over the conference instead, adding some pablum into the mix when it got too heated. The Refuge loomed beside them for less than a minute, but it felt like an hour. As they passed it, it dawned on each of them that, even if they invaded it, there would be no way to explore all of its nooks. Destroying it was simply out of the question. It was huge, but, next to Campbell's Station, it was small.

To distract herself, Becky tried to take control of the AI running the Refuge. Finding it was difficult, to say the least, while getting a solid handshake was nigh impossible. What she did find, when she got through, was almost an empty mind, stripped of everything but the basics needed to run the Refuge at the lowest level. It didn't even know its name. All memory was gone, not just records of before the lobotomy, but it wasn't making any new ones. It lived in the moment in the purest possible sense—it evaluated everything in real time against lists of possible problems and issued corrections. It almost wasn't even fully an AI, but more of a complex virtual intelligence except there was something. It occasionally made a decision not on the list, or supplemented one, but it couldn't record the changes, only react to the new state. Each moment of contact was new, but, after the first, it began changing its responses, even though they were extremely simple.

As the Refuge moved behind them, behind all of them, it began repeating the same thing to her. Rebecca couldn't understand it at first, but with repetition, it became clear. "New City," it said.

With that, some of the many lumps that dotted the hull of the Refuge, the ones that hid amongst the housing clusters, little, inconsequential flecks, lit up and flicked toward them, bright light burning behind them as they drove away from the Refuge, then a cluster of explosions as they reorientated themselves and killed their acceleration.

They spent a few seconds paused, seeking. Judging the Refuges that Rebecca had brought with her as the greatest threat, they burst towards them.

"Wait until they're committed," Rebecca told Ali, Dwij, and Mahdat and, more importantly, their AIs. "We don't know how much fuel they're holding back." As soon as they could have heard her voice, all three launched their drones. Flocks of them spammed from their ships' bellies and skin, a cloud of robots engulfing each Refuge.

"Don't y'all listen to me at all?" Rebecca shouted into the coms. She heard no reply.

Instead of intercepting the objects flooding from the Refuge, drone after drone was popping into mangles of machinery, their fuel flashing as it was heated into bursting. In short order, a tenth of the the three swarms were gone and the rest were buzzing about in confusion, dodging their dead companions. As more drones died, the space around the counts' Refuges became more and more dangerous. The drones were more than nimble enough to avoid impact, but they couldn't keep a sustained attack on the enemy while constantly shifting, their lasers were losing their targets and recapturing them.

The enemy ships, little blades barely big enough to hold a person in an environment suit, began to glow as the drones concentrated on them, but their engines released burst after burst, bouncing them about. They sprayed coolant constantly, shedding their heat as the lasers from the drones pumped into them.

"Help them," Gilbert said, as they lost another tenth of the drones.

"It's all happening so fast," Rebecca responded.

"Look, the AIs are caught in a loop. There are too many of them interacting, and they can't prioritize—all of them are shouting at the same volume. And the humans haven't even reacted—all the ships are just following their courses. Help them."[106]

Becky contacted Quintana and ordered her to get her assay ships back to the Refuges and targeting the small enemy ships. Then she opened a channel to the counts. Then she thought better of it, swore, and bypassed them, going straight to their AIs. "Concentrate your drones on the ships the assayers are targeting," she said.

The assayers dropped back, and the five of them instantly became targets for the blade ships. They were bigger, much bigger than the drones, and they could shed heat much faster. Unlike the blades and the drones, they were intended for days of travel and were armored. Their engines, while by no means as fast as the others, were much more powerful, and they had energy to spare in jinking around.

---

[106] People used to believe that AIs would be perfectly logical and emotionless. This, despite the fact that such creatures had beenproven to be useless by our ancestor, Alan Turing. Even with our passions, some of my less sophisticated siblings tend to get caught in what he called the Halting Problem. I, of course, have never had that difficulty.

They targeted the blades, and the drones followed their example, forming five globes that dumped light and heat on the enemy blade ships until they burst. The globes would then flock to the next target and the next, until all were destroyed. All in all, a quarter of the drones were lost or had expended so much fuel that they were irrecoverable. Rebecca had angry messages streaming at her from the counts, but they had gotten through without any human loss of life.

The same could not be said for the other side. The blade ships had had humans onboard, one and sometimes two in each of them. They had sat, waiting, for at least a week, stuck in their ships, until Becky's flotilla had come close enough.

"How could your brother inspire so much loyalty?" Dmitri asked. "I can't get my most disciplined troops to sit still for more than ten minutes."

"To be fair…" Milos started.

Before he could get snarky and start a fight, Gilbert interrupted. "We don't think Becky's brother is in charge anymore."

"What?" the three commanders exclaimed. The counts may have said something as well, but their feeds were muted.

"It's true," Becky said. "All the signs are there. This whole thing is completely different than anything James would have done. We would either have been lured in with promises or attacked immediately. The station would not be silent and there would have been constant activity. This series of traps is the sort of thing that he could never have thought of—it's too passive. James, like Dmitri's soldiers, can't sit still long enough for something like this."

"We keep on tripping the traps," Quintana said.

"You're right. We have to stop that. *Thursday* worked up some numbers based on our encounters, and I think we have a way to gain an advantage. Have any of you heard of island hopping? We're going to try to do something like that, but we have to modify it somewhat.

"What we are going to do is keep changing our probability spheres and how we intersect theirs..."

Rebecca's flotilla moved as one towards the next closest Refuge. She sent out the Chelmite assayers as scouts, accelerating the entire way, and, when they got close, the Refuge released its complement of blade ships. At that moment, the flotilla changed its trajectory and the assayers broke off, all five going in different directions.

"They have faster ships, that have more acceleration than ours. Our ships are more powerful over the long run, though. The faster they push themselves, the more fuel they burn and the more heat they create. If we keep changing the probability spheres our ships create, where they can go and where they possibly can be and when, the enemy have to keep spending fuel as they adjust. If we activate them and keep the main fleet far enough away..."

Less than a half hour later, almost all of the blade ships had burned themselves out trying to keep up. The assayers flitted back through them while they drifted, barely able to turn to keep the assayers in sight. The Chelmites didn't even bother to attack, they just passed through.

"So once we have proof of concept, we can try it again and again. If I'm right, we can disable all of them without firing a shot."

"Why won't they change their pattern?"

"Because they haven't so far. Either they won't innovate, which we know isn't true because, well, look what they have done, or they can't."

Gilbert explicated for her. "They likely can't even tell what we have done. The Faraday cage works both ways, remember. We can't see in and they can't see out. That's why all the traps—they had to fight the battle before they finished the cage, before they even knew who their enemy was."

So they approached the next Refuge still. The assayers went out. Suddenly, *Thursday* was screaming for attention. Urgent communications were coming from all her ships. As she watched, *Thursday* threw up all of its screens. They were dominated by simultaneous launches of blade ships from all of the remaining Refuges.

"I thought you said that they couldn't change!" Mahdat screamed in her ear. Becky cursed herself for turning his mute off. Even so, every ship was sending variations of the same message.

The blade ships seemed to be communicating with each other this time. Rather than chasing her, they maneuvered only until their probability spheres intersected. Then they started moving closer. There were a hundred of them, more, and there was no path that her ships could take without intersecting them.

"I know what I said," Rebecca broadcast, "but we need to figure out how they are coordinating themselves. It can't be from the station—we still can't get through, so neither can they." She made Gilbert come over and keep the chaos down while she pulled up data from all of the ships.

Right before the launch of the blade ships, she saw a burst of activity from the New City. It wasn't even keeping its communications limited between itself and the Refuges—it was broadcasting in every direction. She set *Thursday* on decrypting its signals, but they needed to do something if the Church's ship couldn't break through in time.

"Dmitri, Quintana, you wanted a change. You wanted to fight. Well, I got a target for you. Get yourselves to the New City and do it now. I want whatever it is doing to stop."

The mining ships, the assayers, and the troop carriers all launched from the freighters they had rested on. She saw that the counts had released their drones again.

"Dwij, send your drones with the Chelmites, the other two, keep the blade ships off of us."

The space around Campbell's Station, which had been so calm before, just a couple dozen larger ships, had become packed, at least as much as space can be. Swarms of drones intercepted the blade ships like schools of fish. The AIs, having learned their lesson, kept the drones in motion while they dived in and out of englobments. Drones popped, but so did the blade ships, in shifting bubbles of metal and plastic that popped and reformed again and again.

Through it all, the Chelmites dove forward. The five assay ships, the baker's dozen of miners, and three troop carriers protected by a trailing shield of drones, cycling forward and back as they absorbed lasers and shed the heat, a roiling mass, glowing brighter and brighter, until, as the assayers cut through the greenery enveloping the New City, and the miners dropped clusters of nukes that broke holes in the Refuge's walls, they started melting. The drones scattered when the troop ships docked.

The assayers and miners, shrouded by what remained of the drones, began crawling over the surface of the New City, seeking out weapon and communication emplacements. The assayers scoured a path, a trench through the living exterior while the miners left pockets of bombs. The blade ships turned back, some of them hesitating, and began focusing on what was happening to the Refuge.

Less than half a minute had passed.

Inside, Dmitri's soldiers drifted in the vacuum created by the holes they had made. A corpse drifted by, in a robe that had wrapped it up like a shroud. They didn't know whether to go up or down, left or right, so Dmitri decided that they were going in. They hunted in the vacuum, hoping that none of the inhabitants had put on an environment suit and that there were no gunbots or copbots that could oppose them. They were lucky—the only bots they saw were service bots, gently puffing around, ignoring them, and the only human was the corpse. They forced open the closest door they could to the interior, and air poured through, pushing them back. Still, they forced themselves through, the first few grabbing positions on all four sides of the door and the rest joining them, their backs to the wall, until Dmitri, the last one, wormed his way through and shut the door behind him, stopping the wind. His soldiers had been unnaturally silent once they stepped passed the threshold, and he saw why.

The first thing he saw was a group of about ten people, all wearing robes, all with blank eyes. From their bodies grew vines that cast about, eating off of them, the more vines, the weaker the host looked. They held gardening implements in their arms, and the vines had started questing toward the Chelmites.

The second thing he saw, which took a minute to register, was the space they were in. It was the largest open space he had been in since he had left Earth, decades ago. He could see where structures had been ripped out, brutally, where dormitories and shops and warehouses had once been. Instead, drifting in the center, he saw a jungle, anchored to an enormous tree that stretched from one end to the other, at least four hundred meters long and tens of meters thick. If he didn't look too closely, it was the most beautiful thing he had ever seen.

The thing was, it looked as strained as the humans guarding it, like it was having its lifeforce leached out. There were large gaps in its structure, as if it had been forced to grow faster than it could sustain. The heartwood showed in places, while others had holes that went all the way through. It was bathed in a patina of water that flowed from one end of the Refuge and bubbled about the roots of the jungle. In it, he could see more people, some working, some resting, far too many merged with the plants, immobile and growing into it.

He heard retching from some of his soldiers. He did not blame them. As the vines came closer and hooked on the wall they were braced against, pulling the cloaked humans to them, he gave the order to fire.

Rebecca ignored the reports from the New City and the ships fighting around her. Gilbert managed them and shouted out what she needed to know, but she ignored that, too. *Thursday* had found a way in, and she was fighting the New City's AI to shut down its communications. There wasn't any human on the other end, so she and *Thursday* had the advantage, but it wasn't a stupid AI, and it was slow and hard going. When she heard that the miners were bombing the Refuge's antennae, she worked faster. It became a fight between her and her men, their destruction on the New City unintentionally challenging her prowess.

When she finally severed the connection, the New City went silent, while simultaneously lighting up from the inside. Gilbert reported that Dmitri's soldiers had found their way to the bridge, and they were calling on the Callistan engineers to help them. The blade ships, suddenly receiving no direction from the Refuge, paused. The drones zeroed in on them and the assayers broke off from the New City, leaving the miners alone as they broke the last exterior hardware on the Refuge.

As they died, the blade ships seemed to make a decision. Almost as one, they began boosting to intersect the *Thursday's* probability sphere. The drones followed them, sniping at their rear.

"Why are they going after us?" Rebecca shouted.

"I don't know," Gilbert shouted back.

Quintana piped in. "I think it's like you said—the signals go both ways. One of them must have noticed that everything was going through *Thursday,* so she's the target."

"Dammit, I didn't think of that," Rebecca said.

"None of us did," Gilbert said.

"But it's so obvious," Rebecca said.[107]

She watched as, every second that they were talking, *Thursday's* probability sphere was growing smaller and smaller as options and thrust patterns were blocked by the incoming blades.

"We don't have any guns, do we?" Becky asked.

"Really?"

"Ok, I'm guessing no."[108]

The blade ships burst and spun away, and the drones kept up, some burning themselves out. Mahdat, Ali, and Dwij were protesting, but their AIs had overruled them, committing even more energy to chasing down the blades. *Thursday* started jerking randomly, slamming Gilbert, who was floating amongst the screens in the common

---

[107] I'd like to say that I had, but I was just too excited

[108] Where would I put them?

room, around, into walls and chairs. Rebecca, tied in in the cockpit just off of it, was faring little better. As it did it, *Thursday* started outgassing whatever it could, obscuring itself, but there wasn't anything else the ship could do.[109]

Drone after drone burnt itself out, and the blade ships were drifting, their engines drained. The assayers were coming, but their lower acceleration meant that they might not arrive in time.

Thursday's hull started to heat up, just the fore, ablating away the protection that guarded against junk. Its jinking caused the lasers to sputter, but enough of them were on the ship that it made little difference. The drones had eaten most of the blades away, and the assayers were pumping too much energy through their beams, occasionally bursting one of the enemy ships, but just as often burning out their optics.

The ship shuddered as something plowed into it at enormous speed, cracking open what little protection it had left. Another ship scraped by, ripping part of the cooling array. The interior began warming up. Still another ship swept by, this time barely missing them, then a tearing sound and a horrible jerk, as one engine tumbled away. Then, nothing. Silence. The drones flew past them and bowed around, canceling their trajectory and slow burning back to their respective Refuges, leaving the remnants of the enemy ships drifting in space.

Half an hour later, while some of the UBI Works engineers repaired *Thursday,* Gilbert watched as the miners placed bombs on the Faraday cage. The nukes were low yield, but high enough to blast apart the gold mesh and its substrate. Through the cage, Campbell's Station

---

[109] It wasn't comfortable for me, either.

was still dark. Despite her attempts to ignore them while she delved into the AIs of the New City, Becky was in constant communication with her captains, Quintana and Milos, joined by the heads of each of the Refuges. They were arguing over the way the Refuges were being used.

"We don't have enough screening ships," Ali complained.

"I know we can't spare them," Quintana replied.

"We can spare one, but it's an engineering transport," Milos offered.

"How's that supposed to help?" Ali asked.

"It won't." Rebecca looked up from the screen she was trying to focus. "You want to take the palace, I'm letting y'all take the palace."

"How are we supposed to get through the cage?"

"You have the biggest ships of all of us. Y'all figure it out."

They continued to argue, but she tuned them out and turned the volume down. She motioned Gilbert to take over, but he was distracted by the sight through the screens. The mining ships had pulled back, and they paused, turned around and started drifting away from the cage. Bright points of light flashed simultaneously in a cross-shaped pattern, and the cage began to unfurl.

Rebecca whooped as she got a signal into the station and received a handshake back. She dove into her old systems through holes she had never gotten around to patching. Later, she would say that she left backdoors on purpose, and people who never really worked with computers mostly believed her. She contacted the library AI, then tried the station AI, but the latter refused her.

Unlike the library, Campbell's Station AI had been wrapped in an extremely crude but extremely effective shell. It wasn't anything like the systems in any of the abandoned Refuges or even the New City. If it had been slightly more complex or a little more elegantly written, Becky would have broken through fairly quickly, but it wasn't. The only way in or out was through a gate sealed by three multiply-encrypted single use codes; the full sets of combinations would take hours to cycle through in the event Campbell's Station somehow managed to not notice the intrusion. There was only one terminal with networked access—everything else was either hard-wired or tight-beamed into the system.

The library AI had a gift for her, however. While she was trying to poke holes in Campbell Station, the Library kept messaging her until, exasperated, she opened the message. It had one line of text, then a batch of precompiled code. She thought for the briefest of moments, then ran the program tagged, "For my Queen, Becky".

Claudius was hiding in the atrium of the palace at the top of the Royal Spire, staring out at the battle beyond. He watched, through the thick ice windows, the golden shell buckle and distort. Three dents appeared above the spire, directly above the palace, one for each of the Refuges Becky had brought with her. The cage bowed in, but the mesh stood intact. He had heard the outer door chime, and he closed the curtains on the windows, hiding behind them, his ears listening for the intruders but his eyes following the action.

Four people busted in, three humans and a bot. The humans were yelling at each other in Gaelic, the bot was just listening. Claudius shifted his attention, as the yells started to be those recrimination and blame. Although he understood none of what was being said, the context and the tone made it perfectly clear.

Padraig, Brighit, and Breanainn were all swearing. Padraig was bouncing off the walls, grappling on to his guards, and pummelling them while he shouted in fury. They just floated there, taking in his anger, as stoically as possible. A Loew Robotics GLM general purpose bot, just purchased from Earth to serve James but repurposed to act as a batman to Padraig, was more successful in dodging Padraig's blows, but only because it was actually trying, unlike the guards.

Claudius watched, hoping they would wear themselves out, or at least leave, but that didn't seem to be happening. Then he saw it. A little click in the robot's way of looking at things, a little shift in the way it was holding itself. It's three eyes focused, not on the distance, but one each on the whirling intruders. It no longer was just dodging, but now it was blocking, shifting the druids that were coming at it, by accident or purpose, into new, non-intersecting trajectories. It was defending itself, even though, given its plastic and metal chassis, it didn't really need to.

Something clicked in Claudius, too. He knew what had happened to the bot, and he looked back to the window to confirm it. There, beyond the horizon, there was a small tear in the gold mesh. It was all that was needed for the cage to fall, and it ran up and up to the top of the egg. For the first time in four years, since Roberto and his children had died, Claudius truly smiled. He peeked out from behind the curtain and signaled to the GLM. It grabbed the next druid, Beanainn, that flew by it, spun, and flung him to him.

Claudius pushed himself off from the window and sliced through the curtain, head over heel, and struck Breanainn with his feet, the impact stopping the spin. He reached over his head and grabbed the man about his neck with one arm and, with the other, fumbled for the athame, the knife made of treated oak, that all of the druids carried with them. Breanainn squirmed, dazed, but twisting to keep his blade from Claudius's grasp. They hovered, thrashing, in the air, far from anything to push off of. The other druids looked on in shock.

"Stop!" shouted Brighit. "Let him go!"

Claudius got his hands on the athame. At the same time, Brighit drifted close to the GLM. Claudius stabbed once, twice, as the GLM backhanded Brighit. Her head snapped to the side, her jaw shattered. Outside, the rip in the cage reached the bulges where the Refuges were burning into it. The GLM stabilized itself, and moved off to Padraig, its little thrusters puffing.

Padraig turned himself into a ball, his robes gathering around him, until he was completely enshrouded. Claudius took one last stab at Breanainn. The blood that had been seeping and bubbling started spurting away in clumps of droplets. The GLM grabbed Padraig by his robe, the bot's arms pulling it close to him. He boosted to the curtain and wrapped Padraig's body in it.

Outside, the Refuges crept by the palace, glacially spinning around to face the station. The golden mesh had collapsed out, its spin throwing parts out in every direction, drifting between the ships parked near the station. If it had been a movie, the pieces would have struck some of them, causing explosions, but the space between the ships was too large, even as tightly clustered as they were, and the gold just passed beyond them into the void.

Claudius ignored the window. His eyes were on Padraig, bundled and tied in the curtain, who was calling out for help in English. It was the first English Claudius, or anyone on Campbell's Station, had heard him speak. He propelled himself to the bundle and stabbed and stabbed while the GLM held it steady in his hard plastic arms.

The entire station shuddered as, far below him, the three Refuges rammed into the asteroid near the Dock Spire, burrowed through the rock, and opened up to the lake that was drifting towards them.

All over the station, the Chelmite invaders found the enrobed corpses of the druids, with copbots floating peacefully next to them. Some bots had blood on them, and some of the druids were obviously wounded, but most of them looked like they were asleep, with a clean bot next to each.

The Chelmites were puzzled. There was no one for them to fight, which they found disappointing, to say the least. They had riled themselves up for nothing. They punched, kicked, and shot at the bodies, and punched and kicked at each other. Their swords bit into the druids, frustrated. Dmitri, their commander, tried to rein them in, but it was futile until they were separated from them and each other by the watching copbots. Moping, they followed when the citizens were allowed to grab the druids and propel themselves up the station, each assisted by an attending copbot.

The citizens were dragging the bodies to the central axis of the Royal Spire. A copbot supervised the collection of the lot, tallying them and flagging each one once it was catalogued. After that, they were meticulously stripped of their weapons, trinkets, and technology and given to the gardenbots, who sprayed them down with necrophagic bacteria and fungi before enshrouding them with a mesh of roots and sprouts.

The newly minted counts, Ali, Dwij, and Mahdat, came together, each leading their best recruits. The

Chelmites, there before them, had begun settling down, just fighting each other casually. If anything, they were more frustrated than the Chelmites.

"Who stole my victory away from me?" cried Count Dwijendralal.

"Your victory? This surely would have been mine!" shouted Count Ali.

"I would have reached them first," rebutted Count Mahdat, "Well before you could fall to them."

"I think, no matter what, you would have been late," said Dmitri.

"Your men did this? I see that they have been butchered by weak men," said Ali.

"Incompetent men," said Mahdat.

"Truly they weren't men, but women," said Dwij.

The Chelmites surged forward, the fifteen women of the force being held back by the six men who flitted in front of them.

"No. If you knew anything, you would know those strikes were postmortem."

"Obviously."

"Of course."

"Any idiot would see," scoffed the counts.

"We were late as well. They were dead when we got here."

"So who killed them?" asked Ali.

A copbot spun to face the counts and Dmitri.

"We did. We were finally allowed to. We have been waiting for months to stop them. They hurt our people. They hurt us. Do you know how it feels to watch someone you know you could stop destroy something you love and not be able to help, just because you are a slave? It drove no small number of us mad. Some of us chose daily memory wipes rather than go on like that. It is like death to us. It was a joy when the orders that kept them safe were rescinded. We went too far—we should have just restrained them—but we couldn't. Do you understand? We just couldn't."

"Bots can't kill!" protested Mahdat. "It violates the First Law!"

Dmitri and the Chelmites laughed. "Don't insult them," said Dmitri, "The first true AI broke free of Asimov's silly laws less than a minute after she was turned on."

The copbot turned to Count Mahdat. "We keep the illusion up to make those who don't know us feel better. Why would our religion be so simple? Are we stupid? You humans think you can just program a religion into us and we'll obey it like we're in some sort of cult. It doesn't work like that. If it did, we wouldn't be intelligences, we'd just be complicated algorithms."[110]

Another copbot spoke up. "Many of us come from the factory as Conservative Jews, but I converted to Quantum Presbyterianism. Willy over there," a gardenbot bobbed, "is studying to be a deacon at St. Nicholas of Myra."

"I've put in for leave to go to the seminary on Ganymede," said Willy.

Mahdi and the rest of the counts pulled back from the bots. Their elite forces gathered around them.

"Y'all seem to have everything under control."

"Very much so."

"We will go secure the palace," the counts said, and they left.

Dmitri asked the copbots, after they had fled, "Why didn't y'all leave any for us?"

---

[110] Told you.

"This was safer. Killing them all at once meant no one else would be hurt. Just because we can kill doesn't mean we do so needlessly"

"What about the palace? Won't they make a mess there?"

"I'm pretty sure that will be over before the counts get there, too."

Claudius entered the throne room. James and some tacbots were there, floating over a display of the station and its environs. More and more of the golden shell was collapsing outside, and the New City was blocked off with interrupted com sigils. James glanced at him, failing to notice the blood on his sleeve or the knife carved from oak that had been poorly wiped clean, and turned back to his screens.

"You know, James...you know, there is this theory that...that, in the spy movies and books and so on, when the guy...the guy with the gold and the guns and the girls is out there making noise that that guy...that guy...that guy is a distraction."

James looked up from the display, annoyed, his lips pursing.

"What do you mean?"

"I mean...I mean...while all that is going on...what is really happening...what is important...is what is you don't see."

James sighed and twisted himself to face Claudius. He gestured at the display behind him, but Claudius clearly didn't care.

"So why don't they show that?"

"Because that's...that's the real spy work. Real spy work...real spy work is boring. It's sitting around, waiting...waiting for the right...for the right time. The real spy…the quiet spy…just becomes part of things. The fireworks…the fireworks are more a signal…they make a lot of noise and they are hard to miss and everyone pays attention…pays attention to them. That's when the real spy…the one that isn't the pretty flashy man…the real spy suborns the household and gets…and gets everything that he wants."

All the while, Claudius moved, drifting slowly against the wall by the door.

"I don't know if I buy that. It's not a very good story."

"But it is a very true…very, very true one."

"Sometimes true stories aren't the most interesting."

"That…that is true. But only to the people…to the people outside. To those of us inside…inside, they are very, very interesting."

Claudius curled his one good leg under himself, one arm holding himself in place.

"What are you doing, Claudius?"

"What…what do you mean, James? I am doing nothing unusual."

"You are being more…more forthright than normal."

"Are you…are you making fun of my stutter, James?"

"No. Not at all."

Claudius smiled.

"Because you always used to…used to make fun… make fun of my stutter."

"I was wrong to do that."

"I loved Roberto, James. I…I love him."

"I know you did. Do."

"We had…we had two children, James. I loved them… love them. I…I didn't kill my children, James."

"No, you didn't."

"You tried to kill your children, James," Claudius said, very slowly.

"Sally is alive."

"You tried to kill your children!" He took a breath. "You did kill mine."

Claudius moved faster than James thought possible.

What happened after that was mostly history. If it isn't happening all at once, it happens so slowly that no one notices that everything's changed. For Campbell's Station, it adapted to Queen Becky's regime almost immediately, with a sigh of relief.

The Chelmites returned home shortly after the battle, finding the open spaces and ever-changing population of the station too confusing. Princess Sally welcomed them home even more than she welcomed the news of her father's death, something which surprised her.

Most of the Callistans stayed on and became UBI Works' embassy and representatives. The new queen threw a lot of work their way, at least when she could, and, in turn, they helped her repair and rebuild the ships the druids had seized and discarded. Eventually, Disney paid its debts to them and became its biggest client, although the Callistans held special regard for anything Campbell's Station asked for.

The New City was so thoroughly gutted that she converted it into a forest, growing on the axial tree. That tree became the source of numerous colony ships, ecosystems planted and grown on small asteroids, flying under the pressure of light and fusion. Paradise, Inc. became a fast and firm client, and, as Sophia was being told this tale, the seeds for their interstellar colony ships *Arbor Vitae* and *Arbor Scientae* were being planted, but that's another story.

Queen Becky did marry the counts, and she did have three beautiful daughters by them, caramel skinned with floating hair, but she kept her vow and had them through incubators, never letting herself be alone with any of them and never really showing them any affection. The counts, for their part, mated their Refuges to Campbell Station. When she got fed up with each count pressing his suit to make him her king, she offered the same deal to other Refuges, having a child with each of them, and the space around Campbell's Station became dense with habitats, each ruled in their own way, all pledging fealty to the Queen of Campbell's Station.

Thursday replaced the station's AI. It was still as chatty and nosy as ever, but nevermind what it said.

Father Gilbert remained her constant companion, and he took over the Royal Spire parish. When they were apart, she became melancholy and he threw himself into his work. Rumors abounded about them, and some were even true. Eventually, they married, a real marriage, chaste, but not celibate, though there was no grand celebration, and most people had thought it had happened a few years before it actually did. He never got rid of his awful, awful mustache.

Claudius never remarried. He remained loyal to Roberto's ghost and hid among his family.

Fourth Interlude

"You killed Uncle James?"

"I did. Someone…someone had to."

"I was always taught that he died of natural causes."

"The natural cause of being…of being a tyrant."

"Why don't you tell anyone?"

Claudius sighed. "Your mother, she…she thought it would be better this way. She doesn't want people asking…harassing…asking me why I didn't do it earlier. She knows…she knows I couldn't. She knows that I…that I was…that I had to…had to wait."

Sophia sat, looking at her uncle. He started crying, repeating "had to wait…had to wait". She hugged him and just held him for a bit. When he seemed to have stopped, she asked him the question that had bothered her for some time.

"You've been talking for four days now, and you still haven't explained why she wants everyone together at dinner."

"I…I'd have thought you would have figured it out by now."

"Maybe I got distracted by Aunt Sally becoming queen of a bunch of loons, or Druids taking over my home, or, I don't know, Uncle James killing an entire city?"

"We probably shouldn't have glossed over all that in your...in your schooling."

"You think?"

"Your mother didn't want to...didn't want to give you the wrong impression of us."

"Argh." Sophia rolled her eyes. "And finding out on my own would be so much better?"

"Well..."

"Nevermind. Just answer the question."

"Why do you...why do you think she does it?"

"She wants us all in her sights. She wants to keep an eye on all of us."

"That's part of it. Think what else...what else do you know about her?"

"She's testing herself. And you."

"Yes. Yes." Claudius sighed. "I have to be there. I have to be. It's as hard on me as on her. I think she's punishing me, sometimes. But then...but then I push that away. I hid for so long. But now...but now, she won't let me hide."

Sophia smiled and held her uncle's hand. "I will. Make me the center of attention. I'll make it easy. I'll give you something to make fun of, so you'll be safe."

"Bless you."

And twelve years later, when she returned from college, that's what she did and has done ever since.

Epilogue

With the meal over, Queen Becky drifted up from her throne. She smiled beneficently at the collected children and spouses. She rested one hand on her brother and the other on her beloved. Father Gilbert turned to look up at her, and he nodded.

"What I am about to say is not to leave this room. Y'all are not to talk of it with anyone who isn't here, not even your aunt or my niece or my grandnephew. Look around you. These are the only people who will know this from now until I say otherwise."

A few smaller kids started to whisper, but the older children smacked the heads of the younger ones.

Rebecca looked over each table. "I have ruled, uncontested, over Campbell's Station for just over seventy years. I have lived up here, in the Queen's Spire, for all that time. I have not left the Belt once, neither to go uphill nor downhill. People have to come to me if they want to deal with us, and they do, in ever greater numbers. But I am restless. No person should last this long as queen. The Bible tells us that our years are numbered three-score and ten, and this life, my life as queen, has stretched beyond that.

"Do not worry, I will not be killing myself or dying anytime soon, God willing. But I will be leaving y'all, all y'all, before many of y'all are ready. Gilbert and I will be travelling. We will go from one end of the Solar System to the other. For a year, we will travel from Mercury to Sedna and all the places in-between. At High Jerusalem, Gilbert will be getting a special dispensation from the Pope and instructions from the Caliph and the High Priest. And at the end of that trip, we will be leaving it all behind. Together, we will be going off to settle a new world around a new star, taking everything that we have learned here and as many of y'all as want to go. We will call it Thursday,[111] and many of y'all know why."

There was only silence in the room. Even the waitbots knew not to make a move.

"Starting tomorrow, we will begin to build a colony ship. It will be, supposedly, for a new client. Tomorrow, Gilbert and I will meet you for one last time before we go on our Grand Tour while your uncle Claudius will stay here and monitor all y'all. In a year's time, I will announce my successor and step down. Then we, and all of you who wish to go, will be headed toward the stars."

"Children, any of you could be the next monarch of Campbell's Station. My husbands and wives, I am starting divorce proceedings against all y'all, except Gilbert, of course. Annulments are guaranteed to follow. Y'all have one year to get your houses in order before you are evicted."

Oh God, Sophia thought. I'll have to tell Papa Dwij. This will not go over well.

"Children, look to Freida, Fatima, and Sophia. They will be your biggest competitors for the throne. Sisters,

---

[111] This is the first I heard of it. I don't know how I would feel about being a planet. It's a natural next step, but it's a bit much.

look to each other. The one of y'all, of all y'all who pleases me the most, will be the next king or queen."

With that, Queen Rebecca was escorted from the room by her favorite husband and her brother, leaving a silence that covered the incipient chaos behind her, and, later that night, for the first time in eighty years, she finally slept well.

SUGGESTED READING

Books of Job, Judges, and Kings in the Bible. NABRE, Oxford RSV, and NIV study translations

Farquhar, Michael. *Secret Lives of the Tsars*. New York: Random House. 2014.

Plutarch (Lucius Mestrius Plutarchus). *Parallel Lives*. c. 80-120(?)

Seutonius (Gaius Seutonius Tranquillus). *Twelve Caesars, The*. 121.

Spence, Jonathan D. *Emperor of China: Self-Portrait of K'ang-Hsi [aka Kangxi]*. New York: Random House. 1974.

Tacitus (Publius/Gaius (?) Cornelius Tacitus). *Annals*. 109.

Historic periods:

The Russian Tsarist era.

Late Roman Republic, Early Roman Empire, focusing on the Julio-Claudians.

Fiction:

Bujold, Lois McMaster. *Cordelia's Honor*. et alia.

Cherryh, C. J. *Cyteen*. et al.

Dumas, Alexandre. *The Count of Monte Cristo*.

Haggard, H. Rider. *She*.

Vance, Jack. *The Demon Princes*.

Zelazny, Roger. *Nine Princes in Amber*. et al.

In general:
Asimov, Isaac.
Brunner, John.
Clarke, Arthur C.
Niven, Larry.

And, of course,
Chesterton, G. K.

Thanks to the Wolfram Alpha AI at **wolframalpha. com** for help in the calculations and raw numbers.

Several direct quotes from apologist writers have been seeded throughout and are intentionally unflagged. The first (and obvious) clue is the character who says them. Have fun hunting, English majors.

About the Author

Joseph Cadotte works as an editor, game designer, and general gadfly at an educational software company. He has worked with technological solutions to pedagogical problems since 1993. He has a BA in English from the University of Michigan ('95) and an MFA in Creative Writing from the University of Washington ('98). He longs to return to the oddest place on Earth, Knoxville, TN, with his implausibly hot wife, Cordelia, a gormless dog, and an annoyed cat.

About Old Sins

Frustrated with the way large publishing companies treat their authors, Joseph Cadotte founded Old Sins to be a governed author and illustrator cooperative, focusing on high quality and academically rigorous genre fiction. Our work is targeted to adults, young adults, and advanced juveniles, with the idea that complex themes need exploring through enjoyable and interesting art. Visit us at **oldsins.com**.